# Sea Sick
## An Apoclyptic Horror Novel

Iain Rob Wright

SalGad Publishing Group
Worcestershire, UK

Copyright © 2012 by Iain Rob Wright.

All rights reserved. No part of this publication may be reproduced, distributed or transmitted in any form or by any means, including photocopying, recording, or other electronic or mechanical methods, without the prior written permission of the publisher, except in the case of brief quotations embodied in critical reviews and certain other noncommercial uses permitted by copyright law. For permission requests, write to the publisher, addressed "Attention: Permissions Coordinator," at the address below.

SalGad Publishing Group
Redditch, Worcestershire/UK
www.iainrobwright.com

Publisher's Note: This is a work of fiction. Names, characters, places, and incidents are a product of the author's imagination. Locales and public names are sometimes used for atmospheric purposes. Any resemblance to actual people, living or dead, or to businesses, companies, events, institutions, or locales is completely coincidental.

Book Layout & Design ©2015 - BookDesignTemplates.com

Ordering Information:
Quantity sales. Special discounts are available on quantity purchases by corporations, associations, and others. For details, contact the "Special Sales Department" at the address above.

Sea Sick/ Iain Rob Wright. -- 2nd ed.
ISBN 978-1479224258

# BOOKS BY IAIN ROB WRIGHT

Animal Kingdom
2389
Holes in the Ground (with J.A.Konrath)
Sam
ASBO
The Final Winter
The Housemates
Sea Sick
Ravage
Savage
The Picture Frame
Wings of Sorrow
The Gates
Tar
Soft Target
Hot Zone
End Play

*For my wife, Sally*

*"The flu is very unpredictable when it begins and in how it takes off."*

–Harvey V. Fineberg

# DAY 1

THE MONOLITHIC CRUISE liner, Spirit of Kirkpatrick, occupied nine-hundred feet of Palma's dockland, its gargantuan bulk floating majestically in Majorcan waters. Its multiple decks rose towards the azure sky and portholes lined its red-painted hull like a thousand staring eyes.

It was Jack's first time aboard a cruise liner, but he wasn't looking forward to it. Most people would have been excited to spend a week on a four-star passenger ship, hugging the Mediterranean's golden coastline, but not him. For Jack, relaxation—and the very idea of enjoyment—was an ability of which he'd lost the use of long ago. The only reason he was there was because he had to be—the decision made for him.

An over-tanned holiday rep approached, her aging skin leathery and loose. "Good afternoon," she said with a Spanish accent. "I hope you all are ready for your holiday. Are you very excited?"

The group of holidaymakers cheered.

Jack rolled his eyes, anxious to get things over with—to get away from the enthusiastic families with leaky-nosed children, and the fondling lovers glancing at him while wondering what a middle-aged man was doing there alone. He was wondering the same thing. Once aboard, his plan was to find the quietest part of the ship and spend his entire week there reading novels and drinking whisky. The other thing he intended to do was sleep—or at least try to. Rest wasn't something that came easily anymore.

"If you'd all just like to come this way."

The leather-skinned holiday rep ushered everyone into a cramped vestibule containing a flight of narrow steps. The steps led up to an enclosed gangway that ran alongside the ship. Jack saw a row of tables with more olive-skinned holiday reps sitting behind them.

The passengers formed an orderly line and waited for instructions. A cheap-suited gentleman came to greet them, a sycophantic smile slapped across his smug, moisturised face. "Hello, everybody," he said. "Welcome to the Spirit of Kirkpatrick. My name is James and I'm a member of the customer service team. If you could all get your boarding passes ready, you will find a passenger number at the top. Can all passengers with a number beginning 02 or 03 follow Karen over to the far desk? Everyone else, please follow me to the near desk."

Jack pulled out his boarding pass and checked the number: 0206606-B. The passengers split into two groups and he joined the queue leading to Karen. Bright blue rectangles the size of credit cards filled the woman's desk.

"Can I see your boarding pass, please?" one of the reps at the table asked Jack. His sky-blue nametag read: Brad.

Jack handed over his paperwork and waited while it was examined. Satisfied, Brad plucked up a plastic card from the table and offered it to Jack. "Welcome aboard, Mr Wardsley. Someone will take you to your room once you are on board."

"Thank you." Jack moved away to join the longer queue that had now formed further along. A wide hatch on the side of the ship had opened and people were beginning to board. Ahead of Jack stood three young men talking loudly and noticeably drunk. One of them sported a ridiculous haircut of shaven lines and childish squiggles, making his skull resemble a hedge maze. He was the loudest of the three, and every other sentence contained profanity. Jack took a deep breath and tried to keep his calm.

Thankfully, it wasn't long before the queue shortened and the three young men disappeared, barging their way to the front. With any luck, the ship would be big enough that they wouldn't cross paths with Jack again.

They had better hope so.

Now a little girl and her parents stood in front of Jack. The mum and dad were muttering to one another as if engaged in a spat, but their little angel was oblivious to the tension. The girl was playing with a life-sized baby doll and pretending to feed it with a miniature milk bottle. Her golden pigtails and rosy-red cheeks made her the picture of innocence.

As the queue shuffled along, Jack saw through the hatch into the ship's interior. Well-trodden, red carpeting led down a narrow corridor before entering a wider area beyond. Midway along the corridor a Filipino woman checked people's boarding cards as they passed. Just outside the ship's entryway, a bearded man stood holding a plastic container. The tub was full of rubbing alcohol, and the man squeezed a small dose onto each passenger's hands as they boarded. The paranoia of swine and bird-flu, SARS, and Ebola, as well as a whole host of other overblown health scares, seemed to increase every year. Jack wondered what good a tiny dose of alcohol would do if a super-virus succeeded in getting aboard. A naïve precaution if you asked him.

The little girl and her parents took their turns with the alcohol, rubbing their hands thoroughly like surgeons scrubbing up.

"Can my dolly have some, too?" the little girl asked the bearded man with the dispenser. "I don't want her to get a cold."

The man was unmoved by the girl's cuteness, but he obliged, squirting an extra blob onto the dolly's plastic palms. Jack smiled at the innocence of it as he passed by the family and into the ship. He skipped right by the man with the dispenser and instead showed his pass to the Filipino woman standing in the corridor. She nodded her head and waved him through.

The open area at the end of the corridor housed an extravagant foyer with a staircase on the right and an ornate balcony overhead. On the left was a jewellery store and gift shop. Jack was hungry, so his focus fell on a pair of smoked glass doors with the words, OCEAN VIEW RESTAURANT, written above them in green calligraphic script. From the sound of it, and by the shadows behind the glass, the restaurant was heaving.

Jack's group was the final intake for the day. Everybody else had arrived earlier that morning or on a previous day. It made him feel like a newcomer to a party well underway. A crew member noticed him standing and hurried over, smiling as he approached. The Filipino man's gawky limbs and bemused expression made Jack think he was unused to greeting passengers, but was trying to make himself useful. His uniform was a light-blue waist jacket with a white shirt beneath, black bow tie, and trousers. Dark hair slicked back, and the beginnings of creases on his forehead put him at a little north of thirty.

"Hello, sir. Let me show you to your room. Do you have your boarding pass?"

Jack handed it over.

"Ah, okay. Cabin B-18, is very nice—a double."

Jack took the man's word for it. He hadn't booked the cabin himself and had expected the bare minimum. If his superiors authorised the extra expense of a bigger room, then he was grateful, but they needn't have bothered.

"Right now we are on A Deck. We take the elevators down to B deck. This way, please, sir."

Jack followed the man, rounding a corner beyond the staircase and entering a slim hallway. On the right was a pair of brass-framed elevators where the crewman prodded at a silver button on the wall.

While they were waiting, Jack asked what the man's name was.

He tapped his name badge that Jack had missed. "Joma. My full name is Jose Mariano Panalan, but you can call me Joma for short."

Jack found himself without a follow-up comment. An awkward silence crystallised, but Joma stopped it from manifesting fully.

"Can I ask what your name is, sir?"

"Jack."

"Like the playing card, yes?"

Jack shrugged.

The elevator pinged, and the doors opened. Joma took Jack by the arm and ushered him inside. "Is your first time on cruise, yes?"

"It's my first holiday in ten years."

Joma whistled in awe. "You must be excited then, no?"

Jack was about to answer that no, he was not excited, but reminded himself that the man was just making small talk, not offering therapy. "Yes," he lied, "very excited."

Joma stared at Jack, drilling into him as if he had a secret tattooed somewhere on his skin. "You not bring your wife?"

"I'm not married."

Joma didn't probe, which was good. They remained in silence as the elevator descended to B Deck. It was a relief when the doors opened again.

"This way," Joma said.

Sconces lined both walls of the corridor and bathed the ceiling more than they did the deep red carpet, creating a strange, yet calming atmosphere. Joma padded along between the various cabins until he came to one and stopped outside of it. "18-B. This your room, sir."

"Thank you," Jack said, reaching into his pocket to find his wallet.

Joma waved his hand. "You no need to, sir. All gratuities included in your fare."

Jack liked the sound of not having to tip. He'd been unsure of the etiquette aboard a cruise liner. It was a relief to learn what was expected, so much so that he gave the man a tip anyway. He'd been preparing to do so throughout the entire week, so if this would be the only time he had to hand over money, he'd still be way ahead of budget. Jack gave Joma a five-euro note.

"Very kind of you, sir. You need anything at all, you come see Joma. He work the bar in the Voyager's Lounge. It very nice and quiet. You have headache, you come to Voyager's Lounge and Joma make it go away."

It sounded nice. Jack thought there was a reasonable chance he might end up there one evening, which made it all the better he'd gotten off to an amicable start with the bartender.

"Thank you, Joma. I'm sure I'll see you there."

"You settle in good now. Have lovely week, okay?"

"I will." Jack turned away and inserted the plastic card into a slit in the door handle, pleased when it disengaged the lock, first try. He usually struggled with the blasted things.

His cabin was spacious, with a private bathroom and living room separated from the bedroom by a curtain. Jack had seen smaller bedsits in his time and was pleasantly surprised by the luxury. Also impressive was that his luggage had arrived ahead of him. His bag sat on the floor in front of the wardrobe.

He had to admit he was almost happy. It was nice and private, and there was even a large LCD television in the room, already switched on and displaying information about the ship. The text on screen informed him that the Spirit of Kirkpatrick weighed 40,000 Tonnes and was powered by two Sulzer LB66 diesel engines. Its top speed was 22mph, which seemed slow compared to other methods of travel. Many more facts and figures also popped up on screen, but they weren't interesting enough to prevent Jack from turning off the set with the small black remote he found on the bedside table.

The bed itself was what interested him. It was a double, and it looked comfortable. He intended to spend at least the next twelve hours there. Even before he had boarded a plane at 8AM, flying two-and-a-half-hours from Birmingham Airport, before taking a forty-minute coach ride from Palma airport, he had been weary. Two years now since he'd last slept through the night, and he was hoping with every scrap of soul that if he could gain anything from his enforced holiday, it would be a tiny measure of sleep. He didn't hold up much hope though. Even now, as tired as he was, he knew the nightmares would not let him sleep. All he wanted was to get through the week as painlessly as possible. No thrills, no excitement, no anything. Then he would go back to the miserable life he was used to. The life he was already missing, for it was his.

Despite everything he had just thought, Jack fell asleep as soon as his head hit the pillow.

# DAY 2

JACK AWOKE WITH a start. The fuzziness that filled his head and covered the back of his eyelids, was a feeling he'd not experienced for some time. The grogginess of a deep sleep being exited. His throat was dry and sore.

He sat up in bed, blinking his eyes. The room was dark, light from the cabin's porthole blocked by a thick curtain. A cube-shaped alarm clock sat on the bedside table. It displayed the time in glowing red numerals.

14:00.

Jack had slept for twenty-four hours.

"Well, I'll be damned."

He pulled back the duvet and dumped his sweating feet onto the floor. He stood up and shimmied around the edge of the bed, mindful of the darkness in an unfamiliar room. The main light was likely by the cabin's exit, so he headed over there now. In the dark, his probing fingers found a set of knobs, and he turned on the light.

The room lit up and everything came into colour. Jack's eyes were still fuzzy, and the sudden onslaught of light made them ache. His luggage lay sprawled against the wardrobe door and must have been what had woken him. It must have tipped over when the ship crested a high wave. As if to confirm his suspicions, the ship listed, and the luggage bumped against the wardrobe doors with a bang!

With the mystery solved, Jack stretched his arms above his head and let out a long, overdue yawn. He had to admit he felt better, as though a storm cloud had lifted from his mind. The world's colours and smells had become more lucid. If nothing else, then at least the cruise had given him a brief respite from insomnia. Maybe his bosses at the police force had been right about him needing a change of scenery. Who'd have thought it?

He pulled aside the curtain separating the bedroom from the lounge and padded over to the porthole. Outside, a lifeboat obscured his view to the left, but he could see the Promenade Deck beyond and the blue-green Mediterranean Sea stretching out in the distance. The water was vast and endless, every inch shifting and rolling with a life of its own. Jack knew little of the ship's itinerary, but he supposed that today would be a day at sea. Which meant passengers remained on board, reducing the amount of quiet areas. Hopefully tomorrow they would hit the coast of France and the passengers would disembark.

Something struck the porthole.

Jack leapt back, his breath catching in his throat. He ended up laughing to himself, though, when he realised it was just a seagull, come to perch on the ledge. The mottled bird stared in at him with beady eyes, then flew away to pursue adventures elsewhere. Maybe he was just trying to tell Jack that waking up at 2PM was unacceptable, even for a grown man on vacation.

Jack let out one final yawn and decided to indulge his sleepiness no more. A shower was the next order of business. The small bathroom was cooler than the rest of the cabin, and a breeze entered from somewhere and skimmed across the tiles. Jack hadn't unpacked his things yet, so he was pleased to see that, with exception of a toothbrush, everything he needed had been supplied. There was soap and shampoo in the shower cubicle and a roll of non-branded toothpaste sitting in a glass jar at the rear of the sink. He reached over into the shower and twisted the knob jutting out from the wall and the showerhead hissed, a freezing jet of water coming out of it. Jack yanked his arm back and tried to keep from cursing. His temper was part of the reason he'd been sent on the cruise in the first place, so he intended to try and gain control over it if he could.

After a few minutes went by, during which the use of the toilet had become necessary, Jack reached back into the shower to test the water. It was warmer now, so he stripped off his clothes and stepped inside. The soothing heat caressed his body and made him shudder. It lulled him back into a sleepy daze, so he reduced the temperature and made the water lukewarm, chilly enough to bring back his focus. He took a few minutes to wash his aging body, getting soap into places he had forgotten he had. Then, once clean and refreshed, he turned the shower off and stepped out carefully, drying himself with one of the plump towels provided.

He crept, naked, back into the bedroom where his clean clothes were still in his luggage. He hoisted his bag up onto the bed and pulled out a pair of long khaki shorts and a nondescript red t-shirt. For footwear, he chose a pair of white tennis pumps. Once dressed, he found himself reluctant to leave the room. Rather than exploring the ship, he could just as easily spend the day reading in bed and swigging from the unopened bottle of Glen Grant he had in his luggage. He'd prefer it, in fact, but it would be ungrateful, seeing as he wasn't the one paying for the holiday. Like it or not, he needed to make the best of things.

He grabbed a book from his luggage—an Andy McNab Thriller-er-and prepared to leave. As he reached the door, he noticed that a piece of paper had been slipped underneath. He bent to pick it up and saw it was the ship's newsletter. Printed in cheap, black ink, as though from a photocopier, it was headed by the day's date—14.10.2012—and the name of the ship in bold, SPIRIT OF KIRKPATRICK. Jack scanned the page and saw it was indeed a day at sea, as he'd earlier surmised. The afternoon activities included, amongst other things, afternoon bingo, a five-a-side football tournament, an ice sculpting display, and an audience with a magician. The evening was scheduled with a production of Half a Sixpence followed by a comedian he'd never heard of. Jack fancied none of the activities, but when he looked at the lunch options he was pleased to see hotdogs would be served on the Lido deck at 3PM. His stomach rumbled at the thought of food, and rightly so. It'd been over twenty-four hours since he'd last eaten.

He folded the newsletter into a square and placed it in the pocket of his shorts. Then he opened the door and stepped out into the hallway.

A pair of elevators lay a dozen yards ahead, and Jack chose a deck at random, pressing the buttons without looking. His blind selection brought him out on the Broadway Deck. It was much brighter than B Deck, with natural light flooding in from an exit at one end of the corridor. A large room-service cart crammed full of stripped bed sheets and pillowcases obstructed Jack's view of the opposite end of the corridor He headed for the exit, the glow of sunlight beckoning. Just before he got there though, the floor rolled beneath his feet and sent him crashing against the wall. He swore and was glad no one was around to hear it. The rocking lasted five seconds and made his empty stomach churn.

"God damn it."

Once he was sure the rocking was over, Jack peeled himself away from the wall and carried on down the corridor towards the exit. He pushed open the heavy, glass door and stepped out onto the Promenade Deck, but was immediately forced back into the doorway when a pair of giggling boys hurtled past like Olympic sprinters. Jack was about to shout after them but stopped himself when he realised there was no point. The two boys had already disappeared around the corner.

Jack took a breath. Keep calm. Not worth it.

The boys turned a corner ahead and disappeared from sight. Jack took in a lungful of sea air and forgot them. The fresh, unpolluted oxygen soothed his nerves. The saltwater on his face invigorated him as he strolled to the railings and leaned over. His experiences of being aboard a boat were few, yet the rhythmic swaying of the water had a placating effect on him. Looking out across the Mediterranean, he felt alone, as if society and all its wretched ills were far, far away. The sea was so calm he wanted to jump right in and disappear beneath its waves.

It could be over.

Jack stepped back from the railing, unsettled by the urges his brain was sending him. While he'd contemplated suicide many times over the last two years, drowning was way down his list of ways to go. Struggling for oxygen and swallowing lungfuls of stinging salt water was not a good death. No, if he were to ever kill himself, drowning was not the way.

A little disorientated, he headed in the direction that the two boys had run. It led him to the rear of the ship, to the Lido Deck, a large rectangle spread over two tiers. At the bottom was a modest swimming pool inhabited by children, while the top level was a sun deck full of sunbathers and chairs and tables. Jack headed for the latter.

When he got up there, he saw at least two-dozen people. Some lounged, while others sipped pints of beer and cocktails at the plastic tables. Jack's fondness for alcohol made itself known as the thought of a scotch and coke made his stomach flutter. While his meals were paid for, his drinks were not, so he intended to take it easy, but with his lack of hobbies and not being a smoker, there would be enough in his bank account to go wild if he felt like it. Whether he did, however, was to be the true test he faced this week. To get shit-faced, or not to get shit-faced, that was the question.

Jack wanted to read his book and enjoy what remained of the sun, so he glanced around for a lounger. There were none free, of course, and it was unsurprising considering the late hour. He was about to resign himself to a hard-backed chair when somebody spoke to him.

"You can have this one."

Jack looked at the young woman, a teenager with blonde curls framing a Nordic face. She was pointing to the lounger beside her and smiling.

"Isn't it taken?" Jack enquired, nodding at the bright green beach towel that covered it.

"I haven't seen anyone use it for hours. Someone must have forgotten their towel and left it here."

Jack nodded his thanks and flung the ownerless green towel onto the deck before plonking himself down. He let out a sigh of pleasure as he eased into the backrest.

"The sun's not that warm now," the girl told him, "but it's better than being in England."

"Where abouts you from?"

"I'm from Leeds. Can't you tell by my accent?"

"It's not that thick for a northerner."

The girl laughed. Her eyes sparkled, and there was a glow about her. "Yours is pretty thick though. Birmingham, right?"

"Good guess," Jack admitted. "I try to hide it. Being a Brummie isn't the most sophisticated thing in the world."

"Neither is being a northerner."

The conversation faded then, as it often did between two strangers making polite chitchat. During the silence, a brunette with striking, dark features came by to take their drink orders. Jack requested a beer—while the girl said she was good—then he shuffled on the lounger until he was comfortable, eventually opening his novel. Before he started reading, he gave his surroundings a cursory glance, more out of bored interest than anything else. An elderly couple kissed and cuddled nearby like lovers half their age. It was romantic in many ways, but Jack couldn't help feeling uncomfortable all the same. Some things were better kept private. Perhaps he was just jealous of not having someone to grow old with himself.

He turned his mind to other things and looked at the pool below. The water still teemed with splashing children, but it appeared one of them—a young boy—had slipped while exiting the pool. The boy's mother was nursing an injury on his knee and rubbing at it vigorously, which made the boy cry harder.

"Were you in the army?"

Jack looked around and saw that the teenage girl was talking to him again. "Huh?"

"Were you in the army?" She pointed to the Andy McNab novel in his hands. "Your book looks like it's about war."

"It is, and, yes, I was in the army once. Six years in the Signals."

"I bet you saw some nasty stuff. Were you in Iraq?"

"No. That was after my stretch. I was still in my twenties when I left the service. The army wasn't really for me."

"Don't blame you. I wouldn't be able to hack it, being screamed at all the time by some dickhead sergeant."

Jack was silent.

"Oh God," she said, putting a hand to her embarrassed face. "You were a sergeant, weren't you?"

Jack allowed himself to laugh. "By the time I left I was, yes."

"Sorry. What did you do when you left?"

"I joined the police force. Been an officer ever since."

The girl's eyes widened at that. People were always shocked when they found out they were talking to an off-duty police officer. It was as though they didn't expect police officers to be actual human beings.

A third person arrived and stood between them—the lad Jack had seen the day before, queuing at the pier, the one with all the lines and squiggles buzzed into his hair. He was topless and displayed a carved set of abs right in Jack's face.

The lad tilted his head. "How you doing, mate?"

"Good," Jack replied. "I was just chatting to your friend..."

"Claire," the girl on the sun lounger replied. She sounded nervous now.

"She's my bird, not my friend." The lad extended his hand out to Jack. "My name's Conner. Who the hell are you?"

He ignored Conner's offer of a handshake. "I'm Jack."

"Jack was just telling me he's a police officer," Claire explained.

Conner took a step back and snorted back a wad of snot. He moved his attention to Claire, acting as if Jack had ceased to exist. "Come on, babes. They're about to serve hotdogs. The lads are already down there."

"I'm not really hungry."

Conner clicked his fingers in her face. "Get moving."

Claire got up and flashed an awkward glance at Jack. She reached and pulled on a long t-shirt that covered her to the knees. Then she shuffled into a pair of pink, jewelled flip-flops. She stepped up beside her boyfriend, ready to go.

Conner sneezed. Sneezed again.

Claire put the back of her hand against his forehead. "Your cold still bad?"

"Yeah," he said. "I'm feeling well rough, innit. Steve and Mike have got it, too. We haven't stopped sneezing for the last hour. That's why I need you to stop lazing your fat arse about and look after me." He went in for a kiss, but Claire dodged it.

"Don't give it me, babe!" She planted a kiss on his forehead instead before wrapping an arm around him. "I'll look after you, honey. Let's go get some hotdogs inside of you."

"Now, that's what I'm talkin' about."

They both glanced at Jack as they walked away—Claire with a warm smile on her face, Conner with an aggressive scowl. Jack kept his own expression plain. If the lad wanted to treat his girlfriend like shit, then that was his business. She'd dump his sorry butt eventually.

He lay back and closed his eyes for a few minutes, enjoying the warmth of the sun on his face. Then the smell of cooking sausage meat wafted up onto the sun deck, and he was powerless to resist his growling appetite. He closed his book and hoisted himself up off the lounger. He was so hungry he could eat a whole pig.

Down the steps, back towards the Lido Deck, Jack noticed something odd: Conner and his mates were not the only ones with colds. Several other passengers were sneezing and coughing, too. A nasty bug was going around. Jack just hoped he didn't catch it too, but by the time he joined the queue for hotdogs, his only thoughts were about food.

\* \* \*

The hotdogs had been good and plentiful, and once Jack had filled his belly with three or four, he explored the ship, surprised to find a sports deck and a casino. His initial plan had been to find somewhere peaceful to read his book, but he found himself unable to settle anywhere. He visited the ship's five bars, chatting briefly with Joma at the Voyager's Lounge, and ordered a double bourbon whisky at an American-style pub called Columbia.

He'd ended up at a place called High Spirits and that was where he was now. The barroom was next to the sun deck, but also, most importantly, right above the Lido Restaurant where they served a twenty-four-hour buffet. It would not be long before he wanted to eat again, and when he did, all he would need to do was descend a short flight of stairs to find an array of snacks waiting for him. Drinks upstairs and food below. Perfect.

His wristwatch told him it was 20:10. There was a comedian onstage, scheduled to tell jokes until ten o'clock. Jack would most likely get a bite to eat after his set finished and then retire to bed with the book he was still eager to begin.

The room's waitress—another Filipino, as a majority of the serving staff seemed to be—brought over the drink he had ordered—another double bourbon, this time with coke. Jack took the drink and thanked the lady before leaning back and listening to the rotund comedian's latest foible.

"The wife and I were sat having a cup of tea with my mother-in-law the other day when, out of the blue, she says to me, 'I've decided I want to be cremated.' I said, 'All right, get your coat.'"

Jack moaned. Mother-in-law jokes. How original.

He sipped at his drink and glanced around the dim lounge. The attendance was high, with all tables occupied. He spotted the family that had boarded before him, the middle-aged couple and their daughter. Their little girl was not the lively spirit she'd been earlier and was now laying limply across her mother's lap. Damp, blonde hair matted against her forehead as she clutched her dolly against her chest. At first Jack assumed she was exhausted from the excitement of being on holiday, but the longer he watched the little girl, the more certain he became that she was unwell.

Periodically, the girl let out a hacking cough followed by a pitiful moan. Each time it happened, the mother ran a hand through her daughter's hair and glanced at the father. The two parents looked little healthier themselves, and as Jack studied the rest of the lounge, he saw that quite a few people seemed under the weather. The sneezing fits he had noticed earlier on the Lido Deck were replaced by a chorus of harsh, chesty coughs. All around him sick people were rubbing at their clammy foreheads and bloodshot eyes, all looking extremely sorry for themselves.

Something wasn't right, Jack thought to himself. There were too many people sick for it to be a simple cold virus.

Jack downed his drink and placed the glass back on the table. Slowly, he rose from his seat, oddly feeling that any sudden movement would be bad. He took another look around the room, making sure that what he was seeing was correct and not an embellishment of his weary mind, but there was at least one quarter of the barroom audience that was sick—maybe even half.

Just as he was about to abandon his table and get somewhere less contagious, Jack was stopped by his Filipino waitress. "Is okay?" she asked him.

"Yes, fine. I'm just feeling a little... claustrophobic."

"You want I bring you glass of water?"

"No, thank you. That's very kind but-"

The waitress shot forward into his arms, pushed with great force. As Jack tried to steady the woman, he saw that Claire's boyfriend, Conner, was the one who had shoved her. A wild spark of anger flashed in his feral eyes.

"What the hell is your problem?" Jack shouted. "What are you on?"

Conner gave no answer. He rushed forward with his arms outstretched, grabbing at Jack's throat. Jack choked and spluttered as the fingers wrapped around his windpipe, but it was only shock and surprise that had delayed his reactions. He regained his focus and stamped his heel into Conner's instep.

But Conner carried on attacking as if he hadn't noticed.

The lad continued to claw and wrench at Jack's neck and even tried using his teeth as a weapon. Jack was confused but not deterred by the lad's ferociousness. He turned his body sideways and hooked Conner under his right armpit, then flipped the lad over his hip in a basic judo throw. Conner went cartwheeling to the floor and stayed there, grasping at the air and disoriented. It was then that Jack heard the screams coming from behind him.

He spun around with his hands in the air. "It's okay, everybody. Just remain calm. Everything is under cont-"

The lounge filled with panicking men, women, and children, struggling and leaping over chairs as they tried to exit the room as fast as they could. They ended up trampling one another. Even the rotund comedian was pushing and punching people out of his way. Dotted throughout the room, several groups of people engaged in frenzied scuffles. The passengers were attacking each other as if some spell had incited them to violence. The coppery tang of blood filled the air.

Jack turned to the waitress, still standing next to him. She'd remained rooted to the spot ever since Conner had shoved her in the back. Jack placed a hand on her shoulder. "What the hell is going on?" He had to shout the words at her, trying to snap her out of the daze she was in. It must have worked because she blinked her eyes and seemed to come back to reality. But the only thing she did was flee, abandoning her duties and racing away into the crowd. A moaning from behind Jack made him forget her.

Conner was back on his feet, preparing for another attack. His eyes leaked blood. It coursed down his pallid cheeks in crimson rivulets. He was snarling like a rabid pit bull.

Jack wasted no time. He drove his fist forward as hard as he could while twisting his pelvis to get his full weight behind the blow. Conner's nose spread wide and exploded as the punch connected. Jack felt the fragile cartilage crunch beneath his knuckles. Again, Conner behaved as if nothing had happened. He staggered back from the blow, but seemed unaffected by any pain. He came straight for Jack again.

Jack swung his fists again and again and again.

And again...

His triceps tired. He'd thrown so many punches his hands had swelled and were matted with gore, yet Conner's shattered face continued to snarl. The lad's arms reached out and snatched at his neck. All around Jack, the room continued combusting in chaos. Members of security had run in to check out the disturbance, but were tackled to the ground by crazed passengers. Jack couldn't be sure, but he thought he saw men and women, who had just themselves been attacked, join the frenzy as if they'd been converted to the cause.

It was time to retreat. Jack could not restrain Conner much longer with punches alone, and it seemed the only way to put a stop to the lad for good was to kill him. Jack was not prepared to do that.

So he ran.

He pushed and barged his way between tables, chairs, and other passengers. Many people were also trying to escape the room, but many more were like Conner, bleeding from their eyes and snarling like animals. Several eye bleeders reached out for Jack as he dodged by them, but their reactions were slow and their clumsy snatches too late. He reached the lounge's exit and bounded through the open doors. Outside, bodies lay scattered throughout the corridor. Numerous adults lay weeping and moaning, nursing open wounds, which bled unimpeded onto the carpets. Those uninjured sought to help those who were hurt.

At the end of the corridor, Jack took a sharp right and barged through the double doors of the Lido Restaurant. The room inside was deserted compared to the busy High Spirits lounge, but a small group of diners occupied the room. Several staff members stood amongst them, equally as confused. Some wore kitchen uniforms, while others dressed like waiters. All of them wore mortified expressions on their faces and obviously had no clue what was happening.

"What is going on?" a burly man in a chef's uniform asked. "People are screaming."

"I have no sodding idea," Jack said. "But we need to get these doors locked right now."

The chef gave no argument and hurried to the doors where he twisted the latch closed. "Okay, the doors are locked."

"Good," Jack said, wishing there was a barricade blocking the room instead of a flimsy pair of frosted-glass doors. "We need to get help."

The chef shrugged. "What help?"

All the people in the room gathered around, looking at Jack for answers. He had none. "I don't know," he had to admit. "What do ships usually do when they're in trouble? Don't they send out a mayday or something?"

"Isn't that planes?" a staff member said.

"No, warships, maybe?" said someone else.

"Isn't it your job to know?" said Jack.

"Hey, I'm just a waitress."

"Yeah, sorry." Jack glanced back at the doors and flinched as another scream rang out close by. "Okay, we shove tables up against the doors and wait until we know more."

"More about what?" someone asked from the back of the room. A female voice.

Jack stood on his tiptoes and studied the crowd. "Claire? What are you doing here?"

"Where else would I be?"

"I mean, how come you're not with Conner?"

Claire moved her way to the front of the group and looked at Jack with confusion. "He and his mates are having a drink in High Spirits. I was just about to join them, but I fancied a bite to eat first. What's going on out there, Jack?"

"Everyone has gone insane," was his reply.

"What do you mean?" the chef asked.

Jack flapped his arms in frustration. "I mean, full-blown, Night of the Living Dead, crazy."

Claire laughed, despite the screaming outside. "You mean like zom-"

"Look," Jack said, cutting her off. "I don't understand what the hell is happening. I just know that we're in danger. We need to get those doors secured. I'm not saying another thing until then."

\* \* \*

"Their eyes were bleeding?" Claire asked once the doors were barricaded. "That's crazy."

"I know it is," Jack said, sighing at the absurdity of what he was trying to tell these people. "But I'm telling you that there's some kind of super-flu aboard this ship, and it's turning people rabid."

"What makes you think people are sick?" Claire asked. "It could have just been a fight breaking out."

Jack looked her in the eye. "There was blood pouring down people's cheeks like tap water. One of them came at me like a goddamn demon. I must have punched the guy in the face a dozen times and he kept on coming. Can't say I liked the guy before he went mental, but I've never given someone a beating half as bad as that and still had them remain standing."

"You never liked him before?" the chef reiterated. "So you knew the guy who attacked you?"

Jack wished he could take back his words, but it was too late. He looked across at Claire and saw the understanding dawn on her face. She leapt up from her chair. "Oh my God. It was Conner, wasn't it?"

Jack leapt up from his own chair to cut her off, but he wasn't quick enough to stop her heading straight for the barricade of tables and chairs that the group had set up beside the door. Before anyone could stop her, she pushed aside a dining table and caused several more to collapse out of the way. She was going to open the doors.

"Claire, stop!" Jack shouted.

But Claire wasn't listening. She unlocked the doors and prised one open, just enough to get her slender body through the gap. Jack grabbed her by the wrist just as she was about to disappear.

"Don't go out there," he warned her. "It's dangerous."

"I have to go. You've hurt Conner, and I need to see if he's okay."

"He is definitely not okay, but that isn't my doing."

"He needs me."

"If you go out there, you will get hurt."

Claire hesitated, half in the door-half out.

"Just let her go," said a passenger behind Jack. "We need to get those doors closed again."

Jack couldn't do that. He pleaded with Claire. "Just come back inside and we'll work all of this out, okay? Whatever help Conner needs, he won't get it from you placing yourself in danger."

She seemed to mull things over. Her panicked expression softened. "Okay," she said. "Just let go of my wrist and I'll come-"

Before she could complete her sentence something seized her and made her scream. Jack had been about to let go of her wrist but now he clutched it even harder, pulled with all his strength. But as hard as he pulled, crying out with exertion, Claire failed to get free of whatever had her, until, just when it seemed his arms were about to fail, she flew into his arms.

The doors slammed closed as the diners threw themselves against them and rebuilt the barricade.

Jack fell to the floor, with Claire trembling in his arms. The girl was bleeding all over him.

"Jesus Christ!" Jack cried out, cradling Claire in his arms. "Goddamn it."

Claire's left wrist was hanging open, spewing blood like a geyser. Her eyes were misting over as shock seized her nervous system. The wound was deep and looked like a vicious bite. Jack shouted at the others in the room to help him—he needed towels to wrap the wound—but they were only interested in securing the doors. They didn't know Claire and were not willing to help her if it meant endangering themselves. It was how people always acted in a crisis. Jack had seen it enough times before.

Outside, the crazed passengers had realised the group's presence inside the Lido Restaurant, and were hammering at the doors. It wouldn't take them long to bust through.

He looked at Claire, wanting to reassure her that all would be okay, but it would've been pointless. She was dead.

Jack looked at the young girl in shock. He eased her down onto the floor and hunched over her, ready to perform CPR. He pumped the heels of his palms against her chest, trying to keep oxygen in her lungs while trying to jumpstart her heart. Now and then, he placed his ear against her mouth and tried to make out if she was breathing on her own.

"She's gone," the chef told Jack, grabbing his shoulder. "You can't help her."

"Shut up," Jack growled, still aware that nobody had offered him any help when he'd asked for it. These people were selfish, and he didn't like them one bit. But he did like Claire. He wasn't ready to give up on her. He scowled up at the chef. "Just shut your mouth and give me some space."

"Hey, she's moving," someone said. "Look at her hand."

Jack looked at Claire's twitching hand. She was moving, but when he leaned by her face there was no breath coming from her nose or mouth. He must not be sensing it, so he moved his head closer, placing his ear right up against her lips.

"Gragh!"

Pain exploded at the side of Jack's head. He pulled away and his ear ripped clean away from his skull. In agony, he watched Claire chew it between her blood-soaked teeth.

Everybody screamed.

Claire twisted and turned, then sprang to her feet like an animal. She looked just the same as before, but Jack could see the wells of blood already forming in her eyes.

She came at Jack with her arms outstretched, exactly like her boyfriend had earlier. Jack was so horrified that by the time he considered an appropriate response, Claire's teeth had sunk deep into his windpipe.

# DAY 3

JACK AWOKE WITH a start. The fuzziness filling his head covered the back of his eyelids; it was a feeling he'd not experienced for some time, yet it was vaguely familiar. The vibrations throbbing through his skull were akin to a hangover, and Jack tried to remember if he'd gone for a drink after boarding the ship.

He sat up in the bed and blinked his eyes. The room was dark. A cube-shaped alarm clock sat on the bedside table displaying the time in glowing, red numerals. It read: 1400.

He'd slept for twenty-four hours.

"Jesus."

Jack got up and moved around the edge of the bed, headed over to the room's exit, where he fumbled for a light switch he somehow knew where to find. The room lit up. His luggage had crashed against the wardrobe and woken him. The ship must have crested a tall wave. As if to confirm his suspicions, the room tilted, and the luggage bashed against the wardrobe again.

Jack felt tired, disorientated—almost sick. Perhaps he was coming down with a cold. He had slept for hours, yet still felt tired. He went over to the cabin's porthole and looked outside. Beyond the Promenade Deck was the vast expanse of the blue-green Mediterranean. The ship was at sea.

Something hit the window causing Jack to leap backwards. He sighed when it turned out to be a seagull perching on the ledge of his porthole. The bird stared in with its beady, black eyes. Bizarrely, he thought he'd met the creature before. The seagull wore a disapproving expression and flew away a moment later.

Jack let out a yawn and went for a shower. It was a strange morning so far, and he wanted the hot water to help wake him up. After months of inadequate sleep, finally getting some left his mind muddled. Once he woke up fully he would be better. He was sure of it.

The small bathroom was cooler than the rest of the cabin, and a breeze seemed to enter from somewhere and skim across the tiles. Jack reached into the shower and twisted the knob jutting out from the wall. The showerhead hissed and sprayed a freezing jet of water all over him, making him curse and yank back his arm. He took a leak while the water warmed up.

His bladder bulged and took a long time to empty, but by the time he finished, the water in the shower had reached a few levels below scalding. He stepped inside.

The heat was wonderful, fingering his flesh right to the bone. It almost sent him to sleep, and he had to lower the temperature to shock his system back awake.

Clean and refreshed, he stepped out of the shower and dried himself off with one of the towels provided, then crept naked back into the bedroom. His clothes were still packed, so he reached down to grab his luggage. As he did so, he paused, déjà vu washed over him. It was like he knew what he was going to do before he did it. He'd had a dream where he'd shifted his luggage onto the bed just like this. He couldn't remember much else. What the hell was wrong with him?

He put on a pair of khaki shorts, nondescript red t-shirt, and a pair of tennis pumps. Then he grabbed his Andy McNab paperback novel and headed for the door. On the carpet, he noticed a sheet of paper had been slipped inside. The ship's newsletter, printed in cheap black ink. It was headed by today's date–14.10.2012–and the name of the ship in bold, SPIRIT OF KIRKPATRICK. He glanced over the day's activities and decided he wasn't interested in any of them, but was pleased to see that the poolside BBQ would be serving...

Hotdogs...

Jack loved hotdogs, but he didn't want any now. He almost felt sick of them, as though he'd eaten a load recently. He headed for the pool anyway, taking the elevator upwards from B Deck and stepping out into the corridors of Broadway Deck. To his right was a room service cart full of towels and bed linens. To his left was an exit leading to the Promenade Deck. He headed towards it, and the floor tilted beneath him, sending him crashing against the wall. He waited for the ship to steady and then proceeded down the corridor, still feeling that strange sense of déjà vu. As he stepped out on to the Promenade Deck, he was almost knocked flying by a pair of sprinting children. The two boys raced down the side of the ship with no regard for other people's safety and disappeared around the corner. Jack was about to shout after them, but stopped himself when he saw it was pointless.

Jack headed after them, reaching the rear of the ship where it opened into a large rectangle spread over two tiers. On the bottom was a modest swimming pool inhabited by children, while the top level was full of sunbathers. Jack stood for a while, enjoying the warmth of the sun on his back and the invigorating sea air. It was the first time he'd set foot upon this part of the ship, yet it was familiar. The people, too, seemed familiar.

He took the stairs to the upper deck. With any luck, there would be a sun lounger free. If not, he would have to make do with one of the tables and chairs.

"You can have this one," a fair young woman said to him as he searched for a lounger.

"You sure it's free?" Jack asked her.

"No one has been using it for the last few hours. I say they've given up any right they had to it. I think someone has forgotten their towel and left it here."

Jack thanked the girl for her help, but then found himself staring at her.

"Something wrong?" she asked, shifting in her lounger. He was making her uncomfortable.

Jack shook his head and broke his stare. He plonked himself down on the lounger and lay back with his novel in hand. "Sorry, it's just... Have we met before?"

"Ever been to Leeds?"

"Not lately," Jack replied. "You ever been to Birmingham?"

"Nope."

Jack opened his paperback. "Guess I'm just imagining things."

"I'm Claire by the way."

Claire...

Jack didn't answer the girl, so she took another turn to speak. "Wait, don't tell me, my name sounds familiar as well?"

Jack laughed and felt silly. He was probably frightening the poor girl with his odd behaviour. "We must have met in a past life. I've just been having one of those days, you know? I keep getting... I don't know, déjà vu, I think they call it."

"Yeah, I get that sometimes. Think it's the mind playing tricks."

"You think?"

A member of staff came over: a brunette with dark hair and eyes. She asked if either of them wanted a drink. It was exactly what Jack needed, so he ordered a double scotch, handing over his room card for payment. Claire ordered a mojito.

"What's one of those when it's at home?"

"It's rum, lime, sugar, and some other stuff. Think it's Mexican or Cuban. I don't drink much, but I guess one won't hurt."

"Have you been to either of those places?" Jack asked. "Mexico? Cuba?"

Claire laughed. "Nope. I had a mojito in Spain last year and thought it was nice. You ever been anywhere interesting?"

"Not unless you count Tipton."

The waitress came back with their drinks, and Jack took a long, eager swig.

"You really are having one of those days, aren't you?"

He gasped, then told her, "I woke up this morning feeling very... odd, I suppose. Perhaps I'm shook up from a nightmare I had."

Claire took a sip of her mojito and was about to carry on with the conversation when someone appeared between them. Jack recognised the lad, but had no idea how.

"Conner?" he asked.

The lad looked at him with a surprised expression on his face. "Who the hell are you?"

"My name's Jack. Have we met?"

It was obvious the lad was confused, even though he masked it with aggression. "You don't know me, mate. How'd you even get my name?"

"I don't know."

Conner turned his stare at Claire and told her to get up. "The lads are waiting downstairs. Let's get go-" A violent sneeze interrupted his words, followed by another, and another.

Claire stood up and placed the back of her hand against his forehead. "You still got a cold, honey?"

"Yeah," Conner said, sniffling. "Me, Steve, and Mike haven't stopped sneezing for the last hour. I feel well, rough, innit. My eyes are itching like buggery as well."

Claire wrapped an arm around her boyfriend and led him away. "Okay, let's go get some food inside you. I'll look after you."

The two teenagers walked away, both nodding at Jack as they did so. Conner still seemed curious about their interaction, but willing to forget it. Jack considered following their lead and getting food himself, but he still didn't fancy hotdogs. He could eat later. For now, he'd relax in the sun and enjoy his whisky.

An elderly couple smooched in front of him like teenagers. Jack looked past them to the pool and nosed the other passengers. There were kids swimming in the pool, adults drinking at tables, and lots of people eating the piping hot sausages. The one family that stood out, however, was a mother and a young boy. The mother was covering her son's knee with a wad of plasters from her handbag, covering up a wound that was too far away for Jack to see clearly. He was positive the young boy had slipped poolside. He thought this, not because it was a likely conclusion, but because it was a one-hundred percent certainty in his mind—he knew it for sure. Could almost picture it happening, despite having not witnessed it.

The next thing Jack noticed was people sneezing. It looked like a nasty cold had found its way on board and infected a bunch of people. So much for the rubbing alcohol yesterday, little good it had done.

Jack reached down and picked up his scotch, finishing it in one burning gulp. As if by magic, the brunette waitress reappeared to take another order from him.

"Perfect timing," he said to her.

She replied in an eastern European accent that fitted her look well. "What is it I can get for you, sir?"

"Same again, please. Where are you from?"

"Romania."

Jack nodded, interested. "Most of the staff on board seemed to be Filipino. You stand out."

The waitress smiled, and he noticed her name badge read TALLY. "They hired me because I speak many languages," was her humourless reply.

"Really? What languages do you speak?"

"Russian, German, French, and of course, English and Romanian. I speak a little Mandarin as well."

"Wow," Jack said. "That's impressive. My name is Jack. It's nice to meet you, Tally."

"I'll be right back with your drink, sir."

Jack watched the waitress walk away and had the sense that, although she was faultlessly polite, she too was having a bad day. There was something about her curt, clipped tone that told him so. She seemed stressed. Working aboard a cruise ship was likely a thankless job at the best of times.

Within two minutes, the waitress returned. The double scotch he'd ordered was more like a double double. "I just charged you for one double," she said. "You look like you need it."

"Is it that obvious I'm having such a weird day?"

The waitress shrugged. "I can sense these things. You give me a shout if you need another."

Jack raised his glass in thanks. "Will do, Tally. Thanks."

He lay back in his sun lounger and sighed. He was beginning to relax. Sun, booze, and pretty waitresses. Maybe the week wouldn't be so bad after all.

* * *

When Jack opened his eyes, it was night time, not pitch-black, for several spotlights lined the deck, but it had grown dim enough that the sea and sky were featureless black sheets. The Spirit of Kirkpatrick was sailing through a black Limbo, an endless abyss. Jack would be glad to see land again.

The tingling heat in his chest told him he'd consumed more than a few whiskies during the afternoon and early evening, and would now be forced to pay the price. He'd intended to take it easy on the booze, but his problem was that trying to stop once he'd started was a battle he always lost. He was on holiday though, so could forgive himself for one night of indulgence. There was little wrong with drinking and falling asleep in the sun.

Jack glanced at his watch. A little after 20:00. Still plenty of time left to enjoy the evening. He stood up from the sun lounger, bones clicking, muscles stiff, and had a quick stretch. From the deck he was standing on, there was an entrance leading back inside the ship. A plaque beside the door read: HIGH SPIRITS.

He headed inside and found a cosy bar lounge, with a small stage and dance floor at the front and a long bar at the back. There was a chubby comedian currently telling jokes and doing his best to make the audience laugh.

"The wife and I were sat, having a cup of tea, with my mother-in-law the other day when, out of the blue, she says to me, 'I've decided I want to be cremated.' I said..."

...all right get your coat.

Jack had heard the joke before and hadn't thought it was funny then. A drink was in order, so he went to the bar and lingered on a stool. Another gentleman sat nearby, nursing a pint of foamy lager. His head hung from his shoulders as though he lacked the strength to support it.

"You okay there, pal?" Jack asked the man.

The man turned his head. His face was a grim mask of perspiration. His eyes were bloodshot. "Uh?"

"You don't look well, buddy. You want me to go get someone?"

The man ignored him and turned back to his beer. The congestion in his nasal cavities made his every breath a thunderous snort. Jack glanced behind the bar and caught the eye of the Filipino waiter who just shrugged and continued polishing glasses. "Nasty cold on ship," he said.

"You're telling me," Jack replied. "Is something being done about it?"

"Ship dock at Cannes in morning. Shuttle take people to local hospital if need. I think is nothing to worry about. It is what happen at sea."

Jack examined the sickly man slouching beside him and wrinkled his nose in revulsion. The man's snorts had lowered in pitch now, sounding more like growling. Jack put a hand on the man's sweat-soaked back and leant in. "Hey, buddy. I think we best get you to the ship's doctor. You don't look good at all."

The man shrugged away from Jack's grasp. His movements were erratic, aggressive.

"Hey, calm down, mate. I'm just trying to help you."

The sick man swung an arm, swiping his pint of beer across the bar and onto the floor. He turned to glare at Jack. His eyes leaked dark fluid down his cheeks, and he snarled like a beast.

Everything came back to Jack at once, like memory capsules opening and leaking into his brain. He recalled the attacks, the crazed passengers ripping each other apart like cavemen and bleeding from their eye sockets.

Jack staggered. "No…"

The sick man kicked his stool away and bared his teeth at Jack.

"Oops, looks like someone's drunk too much over there," said the comedian from the stage. "Don't worry, mate. Rehab is for quitters, anyway. Give my regards to the floor."

Jack put his palms out as the sick man took a step towards him. "Stay back."

But the man did not stay back. He rushed at Jack with his arms outstretched, his teeth bared. Jack sidestepped and slid out his leg, tripping his rabid attacker to the floor where he landed in a heap.

The sound of laughter ignited the audience as the comedian made another joke at the sick man's expense, but then came the sound of screams. Someone else being attacked.

The man Jack had tripped climbed up off the floor. Jack kicked the arms out from under him and sent him sprawling back onto his face. The screams in the room grew in number.

Jack spun around to see Conner attack a waitress while bystanders fought to pull him off her. There were other pockets of the audience that erupted, too, as scuffles and fighting took over. He needed to get out of there. Things were about to get bad—he remembered. He'd seen it happen before.

He ran.

As confusing memories continued coming back to him, the layout of the ship became familiar. The corridor leading away from High Spirits would take him down a set of stairs to the Lido Restaurant. The young blonde girl, Claire, would be inside, along with other people. There was no way Jack should be able to know that, but he did. He was sure.

As he fled down the corridor and took the stairs, Jack discovered that his innate knowledge of the ship was correct. He skidded to a stop in front of the Lido Restaurant's doors and waited outside, wondering whether to go inside. Things inside the restaurant hadn't turned out so well for him last night if he remembered. Then Jack considered the absurdity of remembering what was going to happen. He was living the goddamned same day over again. The more he thought about it, the closer to insanity he verged. With no other plan, he barged inside the Lido Restaurant. He recognised every single person there, and they looked back at him anxiously, not knowing what was going on outside other than that it was causing a lot of screaming. Jack locked the doors and dragged the nearest table over.

"What are you doing?" asked a man in a chef's uniform.

"We need to make sure these doors stay closed. There's been an outbreak or something. People are sick, crazy."

Was he sick and crazy, too?

The group of people inside the restaurant panicked. Jack remembered how they had refused to help him when he had needed their help. He'd been trying to help someone who was hurt.

The girl.

"Claire!" Jack shouted into the crowd, not seeing her but knowing she was there. She appeared at the front of the group a moment later, looking afraid and confused, yet less panicked than the others. "You're that man from earlier?"

"Yes, I am. I'm a police officer, and I need your help. We need to get every table we can in front of this door. We've got about two minutes before people try to smash their way in."

"What people?" the chef asked, looking at Jack like he was a madman.

"The infected passengers. Whatever is wrong with them has made them psychotic."

"You're the one that's psychotic," Claire shouted. Her opposition surprised Jack. "You were acting like a weirdo earlier, too. Going on about déjà vu and knowing Conner's name without him even telling you. Who are you?"

The chef put a hand up to Jack. "I think you need to sit down, sir, and allow us to get security."

The man moved toward the doors, but Jack stepped in his way. Despite being the smaller of the two men, he could take the chef down if he wanted to. "If we don't get this door secured," he said, "people are going to get hurt."

The chef leaned forwards and placed his face right up against Jack's. "Is that a threat?"

Jack put his hands up in supplication and said, "Just trust me, okay? Please."

"Sorry, I can't do that, sir. Please move aside."

"No."

The chef made a grab for Jack but found himself twisted into a combined armlock and chokehold.

"Do I need to put you to sleep," Jack asked.

The chef hissed with pain. "Let go of me."

"I can't do that, buddy. I need that door barricaded. Claire? Claire, listen to me. Start dragging tables over here in front of the doors. Anyone who wants to be useful should help her."

Claire huffed, but did as he asked. The elderly couple Jack had seen smooching on the sun deck helped her too, and together they slid several tables across the floor. The rest of the group stood frozen, doing nothing to help.

"You need to get it right up against the door," Jack shouted, pointing to the tables.

Claire glared at Jack, and her intentions became clear. She did not trust him and didn't want to help anymore. She had other ideas.

Jack let go of the chef and shouted. "Claire, don't!"

His plea went ignored.

Claire unlocked the doors and pushed aside the nearest table, tipping it onto its side, and then she opened the restaurant to the crowd outside.

An eye bleeder spotted her and raced towards her. An older man. He pounced on her and grabbed her in a tight embrace, tearing out her throat with his teeth. Claire's body was limp and dying as a thick torrent of blood exploded from her jugular and filled the air with a fine red mist. More eye bleeders flowed into the restaurant. The elderly couple were the next to be attacked.

The old man stood in front of his wife, but his defiance went ignored as the flesh of his cheek tore free between the teeth of an infected teenager. Both the old man and his wife were dead within minutes, ripped apart like two leathery fillet steaks. The eye bleeders moved on to other victims.

Jack had backed away to the far side of the room by then. His instincts urged him to help the screaming, scared victims, but he had no idea how. He'd tried to protect the people in the restaurant, but they had turned against him. They weren't his responsibility anymore.

He looked around the room and searched for a way out. A throng of thrashing bodies blocked the restaurant's entrance, but the area behind the buffet train led to a staffroom or kitchen. There was no telling what was behind the door for sure, but it was the only viable destination, so Jack sprinted through the restaurant, barging aside anyone who got in his way. He made it to the door behind the buffet train.

It turned out that there was a kitchen inside. A simple and confined area with no other exits or ways out. If the eye bleeders found him hiding inside, there was nowhere to run. He'd cornered himself.

Jack ransacked the room, looking for a weapon. He yanked out drawers and pulled open cupboards, but found only crocks and useless cutlery. Just when frustration and despair set in, his eyes fell upon what he was looking for. In the centre of the room was an island, and hanging above it, a selection of industrial knives. Jack grabbed the largest one he could find: a 12-inch chef's knife. It felt good in his hand. Hefty.

He crouched in the centre of the room, eyeing the doorway. His breathing threatened to become a loud pant, so he concentrated on slowing it down.

The screaming outside faded.

And then stopped.

The sound of silence took hold, and a sense of foreboding took its place.

Jack waited in silence. Waited and waited.

Eventually, his curiosity got the better of him, and he crept towards the door, knife held out in front of him. He reached the door and stopped still, listening for anyone who may be standing on the other side. The first person to attack him would get the knife in their groin, but he didn't know how he planned on dealing with the second and third.

He placed his hand against the door and eased it open. When it was several inches ajar, he peered out through the gap. The narrow view he had of the room showed nothing but overturned chairs and tables. He edged himself through the gap in the door, keeping the knife out in front of him. Blood and bits of flesh soaked the room—a severed hand lay on one of the buffet carts—but there were no bodies. Several tables and chairs had been tipped over, and the blood pools grew thicker the closer Jack got to the restaurant's entrance—the puddles deep enough that whoever shed the blood must be dead.

Still Jack could see no bodies.

Where the hell was everybody? Was it possible that the situation had been dealt with? Jack didn't know what sort of security a cruise liner used, but it had to be competent with so many passengers to protect. A brief flash of memory reminded him of what happened the last time—the first time he'd been through this madness. Security had failed to control the chaos in High Spirits. He held little hope they had done any different now.

The double doors of the restaurant were closed again. Blood and dirty handprints smeared the frosted glass. He opened the doors, stepping into the hallway where he found more blood. It was over everything. The entire ship had turned into a scene from a horror movie massacre.

Jack headed away from the Lido Restaurant and towards the Sport Deck at the front of the ship. He passed by the upper level of the Broadway Lounge, with its balconied seats looking down on an empty theatre stage. There was less blood in there, but it was deserted like everywhere else.

Jack's stomach churned, his senses telling him to get the hell out of there, even if it meant jumping in the sea.

Outside of the Broadway Lounge, a short hallway led to staircases on either side. It led to an area outside with tennis courts and a 5-v-5-football pitch inside a Perspex enclosure. Technically, he had never been there, and shouldn't know a thing about it, but he remembered it in perfect detail. The first time he'd lived through this day, he had explored the ship. The knowledge hadn't left him.

Jack stepped onto the Sports Deck and groaned. It was laid out exactly as he remembered it—with two tennis courts, a basketball D, and the enclosed football pitch—but this time the tennis courts were swamped by a seething mass of bodies. All of them were eye bleeders, hundreds of them, both passengers and staff. The entire mob was focused on the Perspex enclosure of the football pitch. They clawed and bashed at it with their bloody fists.

Screaming children and terrified adults filled the enclosure. The doors were locked from the inside, and the hard plastic walls were withstanding the assault for now, but it would only be a matter of time until the sheer weight of bodies uprooted it. Even now, Jack could see the structure swaying to and fro as its bolted foundations loosened.

There was nothing Jack could do. He was a capable fighter, but no man could take on a hundred crazed attackers. There was no choice but to get the hell out of there, no choice but to leave the children to their fate.

He backed away, not wanting to draw the infected mob's attention. If a single one of them turned around and saw him, he was done for.

As Jack crept backwards, his back hit against something.

The equipment rack, full of tennis racquets, went crashing onto its side. Jack froze.

Up ahead, each of the infected people turned, one by one, until two hundred bleeding eyes stared right at Jack.

The mob let out a screech.

Then it came for him.

Jack sprinted and barged his way back inside the ship, colliding with the walls as his panicked run played havoc with his balance. He took a right turn and leaped down a flight of stairs, heading back towards the Broadway Deck. He had to find help, or at least somewhere he could hole-up until rescue arrived. His instinct to fight was non-existent, and he wanted only to find somewhere he could curl up on the floor and close his eyes until it was over. Jack had never been a coward before, but right now he was as full of fear as a human being could be.

Jack reached the bottom of the stairs and flung himself so hard he almost fell. He was forced to stop before he'd even taken a few steps.

Infected passengers filled the foyer. Blood covered the carpets and walls like thick industrial paint.

He was in hell. He had died in the line of duty, stabbed by a drug-dealing scumbag, and was now on a boat to hell.

The infected passengers looked upon Jack and let out a collective screech. Jack fled back towards the staircase, taking the steps two at a time as the screams of a hundred demons followed behind him. Halfway up, Jack was met by the infected passengers from the Sports Deck. They stumbled down the stairs towards him, tripping and rolling together like a grizzly snowball. Jack found himself trapped as attackers came from both above and below him. A rat caught in a corridor.

There was nothing he could do as the bodies enveloped him, teeth ripping into his flesh and rending it from his bones. He wouldn't have thought it would take so long to die, but it felt like hours.

## Day 4
Jack woke up screaming. The day ended the same way.
## Day 5
Jack stayed in bed all day afraid to leave his cabin. At midnight he fell asleep...
## Day 6
... and woke up at 1400hrs. The day was still the same.
## Day 64
Jack threw himself overboard.
## Day 65
He woke up in bed. The day was still the same.
## Day 77
Jack killed himself a dozen different ways in the following days.
## Day 89
But he always woke up in bed. The day was always the same.
## Day 99
Jack prayed to God.
## Day 100
His prayers went unanswered.

# DAY 101

JACK ROSE OUT of bed, woken by his luggage falling against the wardrobe for the hundredth time. The clock read: 1400 as it always did. Like a robot, he walked across the room, went for a shower, and then got dressed. Some days he stayed in bed, staring at the ceiling for hours and hours until, inexplicably, he would fall asleep at midnight. There was never any fighting it. Some days he attempted to get up and do something, but no matter what he did, the day would always end in the same agonising way—being ripped apart by a mob of snarling lunatics.

The eye bleeders appeared every night, always between 2000hrs and 2100hrs. The High Spirits lounge was the first place to turn bad. Conner and the little girl with the dolly were always the first to attack. Few places held out for long. Jack's investigations had proven that Carlo's Casino on the Eagle Deck became overrun with infected passengers at around the same time as High Spirits, and the two infected mobs would converge on the other places between. The safest place to be, Jack discovered, was in the lower decks of the ship, where frightened passengers remained locked up in their cabins. He did not understand how the infection had got on board, but it was clear from the moment he woke up each morning that it was too late to help anybody. As soon as he left his room and explored the ship, he would notice people sneezing and coughing, growing pale and sickly. The little girl with pigtails seemed to be the worst, further ahead in her condition than everyone else. Perhaps she was the originator. Patient Zero, or whatever they call it.

Jack had once disgusted himself by almost throwing the little girl overboard one morning, but had soon found that he lacked the ability to commit such a heinous act. He doubted it would help anyway. The virus had already taken a firm hold on the ship by the time he woke up. The passengers were doomed, and only he knew it. In a way, that made him the most damned of all. He was alone in the misery of knowing what was to come each and every day. He could warn nobody, and would only be taken seriously once it was too late.

Today, as Jack stepped out of the elevator onto the Broadway Deck, and glared at the room service cart to his right. He hated that goddamn cart.

He walked towards the entrance to the Promenade and braced his legs as the ship rolled. He hardly noticed the sudden movement anymore, so ingrained was it in his routine. The ship's movements had become as predictable as his heartbeat.

Jack opened the door to the deck outside and turned to his right. "Slow down!" he shouted as the two young boys sprinted by him. They slowed for a second but then sped up back to their original speed as soon as they were far enough away, racing towards the pool. The little brats took no notice. Jack had come to despise them.

On the Lido Deck, the usual people were present. The same children swam in the pool. The same parents drank beer and read their trashy autobiographies. The same smiling staff carried their over-stacked serving trays.

Jack went up the steps to the sun deck and threw aside the green towel that covered the sun lounger he now thought of as his. Claire watched him as he dumped himself down.

"You okay?" she asked him. "You look upset."

Jack forced a smile. "I'm fine. How about you? Missing Leeds?"

"Huh? How did you...?"

"Your accent," he said.

"Didn't realise it was that thick. You're from-"

"Birmingham. Yes, well done."

"Funny, how you meet all different people on holiday, isn't it? Are you here with your wife?"

"No," Jack said. "Work sent me."

"I wish I had a job that sent me on cruises. What do you do?"

"I'm a police officer."

Claire seemed confused. "I don't understand. Why would you be sent on a cruise?"

"Because I had a nervous breakdown," Jack replied, for he realised it didn't matter what the girl knew or didn't know about him. She wouldn't remember a thing this time tomorrow.

To his surprise, Claire acted concerned. "That's terrible," she said. "My brother had one of those when he was younger. He has an anxiety disorder and has to take pills. I'm not surprised people struggle to cope with the world when it's such a horrible place. I hope you get through it."

Jack studied the girl to see if she was genuine. She appeared to be. "That's a compassionate thing to say to a stranger."

"Like I said, my brother has been through something similar. I know how horrible it can be. If we were all a little nicer to strangers, then perhaps we'd be happier."

Jack was wary, but couldn't help liking the girl. Every time he spoke to Claire, they had a fresh conversation, and he ended up learning something new about her. The more he learned, the more he realised what a caring, strong-minded woman she was. What he didn't understand, though, was why her boyfriend, Conner, had such a hold on her. In the various encounters Jack had with the couple, Conner would always order Claire around as if she were his slave. Claire let him and was always nervous. There was something going on there, but Jack hadn't yet learned what. Trying to find out would be a waste of his time. It wasn't as though he could change things.

As if on cue, Conner appeared and did his little routine about the hotdogs and being ill. Claire followed him and the two of them went downstairs. Everything was always the same, like clockwork. Events could vary somewhat, due to whatever involvement he took in them, but nothing was ever really different. The night always ended the same way. The morning always started anew.

Jack took a nap, knowing with certainty that he would wake up at 8PM, alone and in the dark, just before the attacks began.

Been there, done that. Got ripped apart by zom-

Wait a minute...

Jack sat up as he realised something. Today, everything was not the same. One small thing had changed. One thing had not happened today that always happened before. Something was missing.

For the first time in the last one hundred days, the brunette waitress with the dark eyes had not come to take his and Claire's drink orders. She hadn't turned up.

She always turned up.

# DAY 102

JACK SPENT THE entire previous evening trying to locate the brunette waitress, but he had failed to find her anywhere. Asking other members of the staff where he could find her had been of no help. They were cagey and distrustful of him. Today was a new day though, and he would have longer to look.

He had awoken at 1400hrs, as usual. The seagull was at the window on time and the shower needed time to heat up. Everything was the same as it always was. The one thing that had changed was the waitress's movement—and, of course, him. Jack didn't stay the same, because each day took another chunk of his soul. He had begun longing for death; all his hope evaporated, but now things were different. There was someone else on the ship like him, someone not fixed in place or stuck in time.

Jack got dressed and headed outside. He took the sun lounger next to Claire and waited for one hour to see if the waitress turned up at her usual time. It was the best place to start—the place she was supposed to be. He threw aside the green towel and sat down. Claire, as always, said hello.

"Hey," he said back to her, glancing around the deck for the waitress. "How you doing today?"

"Good, thanks. The sun has been out most of the day, but I think it's going in soon. Should have come earlier in the year. The days are too short in October."

"Why didn't you come earlier?" Jack asked her before glancing around for the waitress again.

"Why do you think? Money. I'm a hairdresser. I could barely afford to come in October, let alone during the peak time."

"What about your boyfriend? You should have made him treat you."

"Conner? How did you know I came with my boyfriend?"

"I saw you together. We boarded at the same time."

"You couldn't have. We arrived separately." The girl seemed freaked out for a moment, but then she shrugged. "You must have seen us somewhere else, I suppose. Anyway, Conner doesn't earn much more than me. He's a mechanic at a place his dad owns, but he doesn't get paid a lot."

"How long you two been going out?"

"Six months. How about you? Are you with anyone?"

Jack thought of the last time he had kissed a woman. "I've been single for a long time. Not interested really."

"Bad break up?"

"Something like that."

Jack looked around the deck again, becoming more and more anxious when the waitress failed to appear. If she didn't turn up, he would have to resume his wild goose chase. Before he started hunting though, he wanted to ask Claire one last question. He wasn't sure why.

"Does Conner make you happy?"

Claire raised her eyebrow. "What? That's a bit of a nosey question."

"It is," Jack admitted. "You seem like a nice girl, that's all. I hope he treats you well."

"He does. Well... most of the time. To be honest, I-"

"Hey, babe, who's this?" Conner stood in the gap between Jack and Claire's sun loungers and didn't look happy.

"My name is Jack. I was just having a chat with Claire, here. Is there a problem with that?"

Conner's eyes narrowed. "Depends. If you're on the pull, old man, then you and me have got a problem for sure. She's half your age, d'you get me?"

"Yes, I get you," Jack said. "Thankfully, there are no laws against chatting to someone, regardless of age."

Conner snarled like a kicked dog. "You cheeking me, mate? Because that would be a mistake."

Jack couldn't help but smile. The threats meant nothing. He knew Conner's fate. "You sure you're up to making threats?" Jack goaded. "Because you're not looking so hot, to be honest."

"Yeah," Claire butted in, trying to stop the back and forth between them. "You look bad. How you feeling, babe?"

Conner turned his attention from Jack to his girlfriend. "I'm fine. Just a cold."

Claire put her arm around him. "Let's go get some food in you. This guy wasn't doing anything except talking, so it's not worth causing trouble over. You know I only love you."

"You better," Conner said, with a slight edge to his voice.

The two of them walked away, but Jack shouted after them. "Hey, Conner!"

Conner turned around. "What?"

"It seems like a lot of people on board have a cold. Do you have any idea where you caught yours?"

The lad shrugged. "I was fine until I got on this bloody ship. Probably just some bug brought on board by a greasy Spaniard."

Nice, Jack thought. He's a racist and a thug. What a catch, Claire.

"Maybe you should go to your room and lie down," Jack said. "It might make you feel better."

"I don't need advice from you, mate. Don't even know you. There's a doctor on the bottom deck. I'll go see him if I need to, but you can mind your own business."

"Just trying to help," Jack said, already thinking about other things. Conner had gotten sick once on board the ship, not before. The second was that there was a doctor on board. Jack irritated himself because he had known that—it said so on the ship's newsletter that came every day. The doctor might make sense out of whatever was infecting the passengers. Perhaps the ship's doctor would already know something about what was happening. The question Jack now had to answer was whether to spend the afternoon looking for the brunette waitress, or seeking out the ship's medical centre.

He eventually decided to visit the lower decks and check out the infirmary. The reasoning being he had no idea where to find the waitress anyway, so there was just as much chance he'd find her there as anywhere else.

The main elevators in the foyer of the Mariner Deck—where High Spirits was located—took Jack all the way down to C Deck and opened right outside the medical bay—a grim, green painted corridor with two offices and a consulting room. There were no members of staff present, so Jack took a seat on a green-cushioned bench running along one side of the corridor.

Voices came from somewhere nearby, most likely the ship's doctor with a patient. Jack had expected the waiting area to be filled with coughing passengers, but he sat there alone.

He checked his watch awhile later, surprised to see that twenty minutes had gone by. For the last several months, every minute seemed like an hour, each day seemed longer than the last, but the last twenty minutes had flown by in what seemed like seconds. Anticipation of learning something new made time abstract and inconsequential. Jack felt alive again, his investigative spirit reawakened.

Someone entered the corridor a short time later—the two parents and their pigtailed daughter. The little girl would be the first to turn savage in High Spirits, but whatever was wrong with her, the doctor obviously didn't do anything to help. Jack assumed the family came here every day looking for answers, but failed to ever get any. Everyone on board followed the same routine.

Except the brunette waitress.

Jack was still eager to talk to the brunette, but right now he had other things to concentrate on. The doctor had just entered the corridor.

The towering medic was dark-skinned and bearded, from African descent. When he asked Jack to follow him into the consulting room, he spoke English well but with a French twang.

"Are you the doctor?" Jack asked as he entered the confines of the small office. A padded examination table sat in the centre of the room, and several cabinets lined the walls.

"Yes, I am Doctor Fortuné. What is it I can do for you, sir?"

"I need to understand what was wrong with the little girl who just left."

"I'm sorry? Are you ill yourself?"

"No," Jack replied. "But lots of other people on this ship are. I need to know what is wrong with them. I want to know what you know."

The doctor seemed irritated and confused. "I'm afraid I cannot discuss these things with you, sir. If you are not ill, then you will have to leave."

Jack sighed. He respected the confidentiality of the Hippocratic Oath—as a police officer, he abided by similar virtues himself—but this was not the time for ethics or convention.

"Okay," Jack relented, deciding to try a different tactic. "But there's something nasty going between the passengers on board this ship, and in the interest of my own health, can you tell me what I should look out for? You have a duty to inform me if I am at risk."

The doctor let out a long breath and relaxed, apparently happy to exploit the loophole presented to him. "Okay, sir. What I can tell you is that there seems to be a highly contagious cold virus aboard this ship. There have been several cases this morning already, but none are at all threatening. It is just a cold, my friend. Nothing to worry about, okay? Wash your hands regularly and avoid touching your face. You will be fine."

"It can't just be a cold," Jack protested. "People don't turn into psycho-killers because of the sniffles."

The doctor looked confused. "I'm sorry?"

"Oh, yeah." Jack chuckled. "That doesn't make a lot of sense to you, does it?"

The doctor stared at him.

"Look," Jack continued. "Is there anything unusual about this cold going around? You said it's highly contagious. Is that normal?"

"Yes and no. Cold viruses are often highly infectious by nature, but the number of cases I've seen today is higher than average. Still no reason for alarm."

Jack sighed. This was going nowhere. "Okay, Doctor. Thank you for your help."

He was almost out the door when the doctor spoke up. "Actually, my friend, there is one thing I find a little strange."

Jack spun back around. "What?"

The doctor seemed to change his mind about divulging the information and looked upon Jack with scrutiny. "Who are you, exactly? Why are you so interested in this?"

"I'm a police officer, and I have a bad feeling. This isn't just a cold virus, I assure you."

"Do you know something I do not?"

Jack knew many things the doctor did not, but there was no way to explain any of them without sounding like a lunatic. "No, I don't know anything for sure," he said. "Please, tell me what you've learned."

The doctor let out a sigh and started talking. "There's something strange about this cold virus. The people who have it are suffering from elevated blood pressure. The later it has gotten in the day, the quicker their pulses have been when I've measured them. It's almost like their hearts are speeding up."

Jack grunted. "Jesus. Isn't that something to be worried about?"

"I cannot explain it, but the measurements are still within safe levels. It's just very strange, that is all. A simple cold should not affect a person in such a way. At least, not typically."

"What would happen if their heartbeats keep getting faster?"

"Tachycardia can cause excitement and even mania, but eventually it leads to ischemia."

"What's that?"

"It is where the heart beats so fast it can no longer supply the body efficiently with blood. The resulting oxygen deficit results in the vital organs shutting down."

"What can be done for someone with ischemia?"

"An antiarrhythmic agent can be administered, but as I said, what I have seen is nowhere near the required levels to make a diagnosis like that appropriate. My prognosis is still a simple cold virus. In fact, I shouldn't have spoken as freely with you as I have."

"Okay," Jack said, understanding he would get nothing more. "I'll leave you to your work, but I have one last question."

The doctor sighed. "What is your question?"

"If someone's heartbeat gets to a dangerous level, how would I know?"

"They would become lethargic and pale. They might also have chest pain."

"If I bring someone like that to you, could you help them?"

The doctor frowned at Jack, probably trying to work out what was going on here. "I could try."

"Okay," Jack said. "That's a start."

He left the doctor alone and headed back towards the elevators. A plan began to form in his mind.

\* \* \*

It was 19:10, and Jack was sitting in High Spirits, nursing a shot of bourbon. The parents and their daughter were sitting two tables ahead. The little girl lay across her mother's lap as she did every night. She was both lethargic and pale.

It was Jack's intention to get the young girl downstairs to the doctor, before 2000hrs when her condition would take an irreversible turn for the worse. Once the little girl started tearing into people, no doctor in the world could help her. Jack needed to get her to the medical bay before that happened. The one thing standing in his way was getting her parents to comply. He was not without a plan though.

He stood up from his table and headed over to the family. They looked up at him as he approached, distrustful. Jack wore his most reassuring smile, perfected during years on the force. It was something he relied on to calm people down when he had little else at his disposal. Thankfully, it worked now, and the family loosened up and smiled back.

"Hey, there," he said in a friendly voice. "I'm sorry to come over like this, but I'm a nurse at the Queen Elizabeth Hospital in Birmingham. I couldn't help but notice how poorly your little angel looks."

The mother looked on the verge of tears. It was obvious the woman was under the weather too, but her concern was only for her daughter.

"She's been ill since she woke up this morning. The doctor said she has a cold, but I'm beginning to worry."

Jack had never had children himself, so he didn't have a clue, really, but he could imagine, and he understood what love felt like. He looked both the father and the mother in the eyes as he spoke. "Why don't we take her back down to the medical bay now? We can get the doctor to have another look at her."

The mother's eyes widened, and she was alarmed. "Oh, God, you think there's something wrong with her, don't you?"

Jack held his hands up and shook his head. "She's fine, I'm sure, but it's obvious that she's suffering. We should go see what the doctor can do to help her."

"Why, might I ask, are you so interested?" the father asked in a clipped, Scottish accent. Despite the accent, his speech was very prim and proper, in stark contrast to the casual idiom used by his wife. His age was at least fifteen years her senior—mid-fifties.

Jack answered. "It's my job. I don't stop caring about public health just because I'm on holiday."

The father seemed to mull this over. "Okay then. Come on, Vicky. Let's take her down."

The mother handed her daughter to her husband and stood up on shaky legs. Jack reached out to steady her, but she shrugged him away and told him she was fine. Together, they travelled to C Deck. When they reached the medical bay, they found it dimly lit and deserted.

"I don't think the doctor works at night," Vicky said, sounding worried.

"He'll be on call," the husband responded. "There'll be a way to contact him."

"There is," Jack said, pointing a finger.

In the waiting room was a notice on the wall. It read, above a small red button, CALL FOR DOCTOR. Jack stabbed the button with his finger. Five minutes later, Doctor Fortuné arrived, looking sleepy, yet well presented in his white lab coat.

"Can I help you?" he asked, seeming to recognise them but unable to recall why.

"Our daughter needs help," Vicky said.

"This man here is a nurse," said her husband, pointing at Jack.

The doctor frowned. "No, he is not. He told me he was a police officer."

So he does remember me, thought Jack, cringing at the position he was now in.

"What?" The husband sounded furious, and his demeanour and stance changed to one of capable intent. Jack realised then that the older man was ex-army. From the tone alone it was obvious.

"Oh, God, Ivor," Vicky whimpered. "Who is this man?"

"I don't know, but he has a great deal of explaining to do."

Jack took a step back. "Okay, I admit I lied, but I did it because I'm worried about your daughter. The doctor gave me some signs to watch out for earlier. Things to suggest that this cold-bug going around is getting worse."

The parents looked confused. Doctor Fortuné shook his head. "Sir, you have to stop meddling in affairs that do not concern you. I assure you that there is nothing on board that requires your attention."

As if to disagree, the little girl in her father's arms moaned.

"She's lethargic," Jack said. "She's pale. Her condition is worsening. Look at her. Look at her."

The doctor glanced at the girl and then focused his attention on the father. "Has she been having any chest pains or bouts of breathlessness?"

Ivor nodded solemnly.

"Okay," the doctor said. "Let's go into the office and have a look at her, then."

The family headed into the consultation room, and Jack went to go with them, but Ivor put a meaty fist against his chest. "I'm not sure what your situation is, friend, but I request you stay away from my family."

Jack could tell it was a veiled threat and decided not to push it. If his plan worked, then the doctor would help the young girl; if not, then the night would end as it always did, and nobody would be any worse off. His sole intention was to find out if the infected passengers could be helped—or even cured. Maybe, if he found a way to save them, he would be released from the hellish prison he found himself in every day. Perhaps that was the reason he was here.

He needed to stay close and see what happened, so he took a seat on the same green bench he'd been sitting on earlier in the day. From inside the nearby office, he could hear the voices of the worried family and the concerned doctor. He looked at his watch: 20:05. Not long left. All around the ship, infected people would be gearing up to explode. There was nothing to lose now, so Jack stood up and pushed open the door to the doctor's office.

Ivor glared at him as he entered, but said nothing. His little girl lay on the examination table breathing in shallow gasps. Her condition was dire; Jack knew that, but he had never been this close to one of the infected right before they turned into a monster.

"How is she?" Jack asked.

"She's tachycardic," the doctor replied. "You were right to bring her to me. I've given her something to slow her heart rate, but it is still worryingly fast."

The girl's mother, Vicky, was sobbing on a chair in the corner while her husband stood beside her. Jack went over to both of them. "I'm sorry for deceiving you both," he said.

"Thank you," Vicky said between sobs. "You knew she needed a doctor."

"How did you?" Ivor asked. "You're not even a nurse."

"No, I'm not. I'm a police officer, and ex-army, like you, Ivor. I've got pretty good at sensing danger."

Ivor lowered his guard and shook Jack's hand. "Major Curtis, good to meet you."

"Sergeant Wardsley. Pleased to meet you, too, sir."

Ivor laughed. "Been a while since I had a sergeant calling me that. Takes me back."

"Been retired long?"

"Good ten years now. I married Vicky two years before I signed out. Wanted to spend time with her. Have a family while I still had lead in my pencil. A few years and we had this little gift from God, Heather."

"Well, it's good to meet you all." Jack turned to the doctor. "How is Heather doing, Doc?"

"I think she is stabilising, but we need to get her to a hospital as soon as we reach port. How did you know this would happen? All of your questions this morning…?"

"I just had a bad feeling. But you've helped her, right, Doc? She's going to be okay?"

"I believe so. As long as I can keep her heart rate under control."

A noise from behind the doctor made everyone in the room jump. It was Heather on the examination table. She was having a seizure, but almost as soon as it started, it stopped. Doctor Fortuné hurried over to the girl and placed his stethoscope against her chest, moving it around frantically. The concern on his face made it obvious her heart was doing things it shouldn't. He performed CPR, pressing on Heather's chest and using a breath pump on her face. He kept at it for several minutes while Jack worried. The girl's parents were frantic.

"Get away from her, Doc," Jack warned. "I don't think you should be that close to her."

Ivor shoved Jack hard. "What are you playing at, man? She needs help."

Jack ignored the shove and rushed towards Doctor Fortuné, tackling the medic around the waist and moving him away from Heather.

Vicky wailed in torment while her husband shouted obscenities.

Heather sprang up on the bed. The little girl glanced around the room like a freshly hatched vulture. Vicky cried out with joy and raced across the room to her daughter.

There was no time for Jack to stop her.

Heather leapt off the table and met her mother in an embrace. Vicky squeezed her daughter tight, tears streaming down her face. "Thank God," she said. "Oh, thank God."

Heather bit her mother's neck, tearing her jugular in two. Blood arced high enough to splatter the florescent lights overhead and cast spotty shadows over the room.

Ivor screamed, perhaps for the first time in his life if his tough military exterior was anything to go by. Doctor Fortuné stood there, stunned, but Jack acted fast. He grabbed Heather around the throat and dragged her back towards the examination table.

"Get something to tie her down," Jack shouted at the other two men.

Jack expected Ivor to resist him, but the Major was more than willing to comply. He and the doctor upended the room looking for something to use for bindings, and they found several bundles of dressing tape and a roll of bandages. They brought it over to Jack.

"Ivor, grab her feet, and I'll get her wrists. Doc, you strap her down."

The doctor ran the tape beneath the examination table and wrapped it up around Heather's body in tight circles. Heather kicked and squirmed, and by the time Jack was done, she looked like an Egyptian mummy. The final roll of tape he used to bind her forehead to the table, keeping her head in place.

With one crisis over, Ivor's focus turned to his wife who was bleeding on the floor. The husband dropped to his knees and cradled his wife in his arms. "Jesus Christ, we need to help her. Doctor, do something."

Doctor Fortuné grabbed a bundle of gauze and bandages and did his best to cover Vicky's neck wound. The blood seeped between his fingers, but slowed a little. The final thing he did was inject her with something, which Jack presumed was a clotting agent. Ivor kept his hand pressed tight against his wife's neck, placing as much pressure as he could. The ex-army man didn't need to be taught basic first aid.

"Is that all you can do?" Ivor shrieked. "You have to stop the bleeding."

"I cannot. I am no surgeon."

Ivor sobbed, holding his wife in his arms. The doctor looked shaken, so Jack put a hand on his bony shoulder and turned him around. There was a small window of opportunity to get answers.

"What do we do, Doc?" Jack asked. "What's wrong with the girl?"

The doctor stood in a daze for a moment, staring at Heather on the examination table. The girl was gnashing her teeth as though she were chewing the air itself. Her eyes were red and bleeding. He placed his stethoscope against the girl's chest, then looked at Jack with a complete lack of understanding written across the creases of his face.

"This cannot be," he said.

Jack stared hard at the man. "What? What is it?"

"She has no heartbeat."

"Are you telling me she's dead?"

The doctor took a penlight from his breast pocket and shined it into Heather's eyes. She snapped and hissed as his hand neared her mouth.

Jack asked, "Why are her eyes bleeding?"

"I don't know. It's some kind of subconjunctival haemorrhaging. Her pupils are not reacting to the light."

"She's not breathing," Jack noted.

The doctor looked at the girl's chest. Completely still. "I believe she is dead," he stated matter-of-factly. "At least, she should be."

"What the hell are you lunatics talking about?" Ivor shouted from the floor. Vicky was growing weaker in his arms. "If she's dead, then how on earth is she moving, you imbeciles?"

No one said anything. The situation was beyond rationalization. Jack stared at Heather and watched her mouth working feverously. She wanted to taste human flesh, and if they unbound her, she would attack the nearest person—it was the biological imperative of the virus coursing through her body, a way of spreading itself to new hosts. An infected host bites an uninfected host and passes on the virus through saliva.

Jack began to understand something.

Passes it on...

Before he had a chance to figure anything out, Ivor wailed in fright. Vicky gouged her fingernails into his cheeks and pulled his face towards hers, with strength twice what it should have been. Ivor was powerless as the girl sunk her teeth into the chubby flesh beneath his left eye. It almost looked like they were kissing, but Ivor's screams suggested otherwise.

Jack grabbed the ex-soldier around the collar and tried to drag him away, but Vicky hung on to him with her teeth. Jack pulled harder until the flesh of Ivor's cheek ripped away. Ivor stopped his screaming long enough to get to his feet, but continued whimpering like a little boy. He stumbled away from his wife and heaved. "W-What in damnation is happening to my family?"

"I don't know," Jack said. "Just keep away from your wife."

Vicky rose to her feet, a puppet on tangled strings. She scanned the room with feral eyes. A moment of inactivity, a brief pause while nobody moved, and then she lunged. Her bloody fingertips stretched towards the gaping wound on Ivor's face as though the sight of her husband's blood excited her.

Ivor probably could have killed most men with a single punch to the throat, but he was unwilling to retaliate against his own wife, so he allowed Vicky to collide with him, and the two wrestled. Jack came up behind Vicky and grabbed her in a full nelson, pinning her arms above her head while restraining movement of her head—and jaws.

"Okay," Jack said, struggling to restrain the woman in his arms. "Ivor... listen to me. I need to understand how your daughter got sick. Has Heather been in contact with somebody else who was unwell? What about you and your wife? You both have it too. Were you exposed to anything?"

Ivor was flustered—understandably so, for his family was dead, yet he found the strength to concentrate. "We came straight from the airport in Palma. We were with a bunch of other passengers the whole time. They were all perfectly fine."

Jack needed more. He needed answers. "You and your wife were arguing the day you came on board. What about?"

"Arguing? I don't know what you're talking about."

"Yes, you do," Jack said, still struggling to restrain Vicky thrashing in his arms. "Does it have something to do with why you're sick?"

"Of course not."

"But you admit you were arguing?"

Ivor seemed to battle with the fringes of despair. "We... we were arguing about what was for the best. I had an old friend from the forces waiting for us in Germany, all ready to help us disappear. Vicky was having second thoughts."

Jack was confused. He'd expected the conversation to lead somewhere else. "Second thoughts about what?"

"Vicky turning herself in."

Jack frowned. "What the hell are you talking about? What did she do?"

Before Ivor had time to answer, Doctor Fortuné let out a sudden yelp. Jack turned his head to see that Heather was partially free from her bindings and sat up on the examination table. She was munching on something, and when the doctor turned around, he was holding out his right hand and trembling. He was missing a thumb.

Jack thought about what happened to Vicky after her daughter attacked her and reached an unwelcomed conclusion. "Doctor, I'm sorry, but you're infected now. You need to isolate yourself somewhere, quickly."

But the doctor wasn't listening. He stumbled around the room, gushing blood from his thumb-stump. The sudden commotion caused Jack to lose his grip on Vicky. She pulled free of his grasp and pounced on her husband, tearing out his windpipe before he even had time to scream.

Ivor crumpled to the floor, dead.

Jack acted, scouring the room for something to defend himself with. Even though he knew dying would cause nothing more than him waking up again at 1400hrs, he couldn't help but fight back. It was his instinct, a human behaviour rooted deep inside him, and making it impossible to accept any death willingly. There was also the fear that, eventually, the spell would end and whatever happened to him would be permanent. A part of Jack longed for death and welcomed an end to his nightmare, but he was finally getting somewhere.

A glass paperweight sat on a nearby stack of papers. Jack wrapped his fingers around it and hefted it through the air with all his might. It cracked against Vicky's skull just as she turned to face him.

The paperweight was as solid as Jack had hoped it would be, and he heard it shatter against Vicky's skull. She crumpled to the floor, a curtain cut from its railing.

Jack had come up against the infected dozens of times now, ever since his first encounter in High Spirits, and it seemed the best way to put them out of action was blunt-force trauma to the skull. Jack was certain of it now.

Ivor lay dead on the floor, but it would only be a matter of time before he was on his feet again, windpipe dangling down his chest, yet still snarling. But there was a bigger threat to deal with right now.

Heather was still sitting up on the examination table, reaching out for Doctor Fortuné, who was frantically cleaning his wound in a nearby sink. Heather, who had just been declared dead by a medical professional, was almost free of her bonds now. Jack didn't have the ability to hurt the girl, regardless of whether she was dead or alive, so he grabbed more tape from a nearby cabinet, and wrestled her back to the table. He secured her without being bitten and was confident she would be held in place long enough for him to get his arse out of there. Not that there was anywhere to run.

He picked up the bloody paperweight from where it lay cracked and broken on the floor and turned to Ivor's bleeding corpse. It felt wrong to bludgeon the skull of a dead man, but it had to be done, so Jack raised the paperweight above his head, like a caveman brandishing a rock, and brought it down on Ivor's forehead just as the old Major opened his blood-soaked eyes. Jack was sorry he hadn't done it quick enough to spare Ivor from coming back.

Jack stood back up. His red t-shirt was darker in patches where blood stained the fabric. He had blood on his face and hands, too. It stirred memories in him he wished he could erase—memories of his partner lying dead in his arms, another innocent victim of humanity's rotten core.

Jack placed the gore-encrusted glass cube on the nearby desk and took deep breaths. Death surrounded him, the room filled with it. He was nauseous and weary, lost in an endless abyss of screaming terror and unbearable pain. Every day the same, however different it might appear to be.

Something clamped Jack's shoulder. His trapezius muscle burned with searing splinters of agony. Doctor Fortuné had turned, and Jack had paid the price for turning his back. He'd been bitten.

He punched the doctor away, then placed a hand to his ragged shoulder and felt blood coursing from his neck. Jack had been torn to shreds a dozen times by the infected passengers—a dozen different ways on a dozen different nights—but he had never been bitten and left to turn. He had to be infected. What would happen?

Doctor Fortuné launched another attack.

Jack dodged to the side and pushed the doctor to the floor before deciding to make a run for it. He flung open the door to the office and sprinted out into the corridors of C Deck, leaving the medical bay behind him and heading for the passenger section of the deck.

When he got there, he found it filled with eye bleeders. They wandered between the cabins, dragging anyone uninfected from their rooms as they opened up to see what the commotion was.

Jack skidded on his heels, but his knees were weak, and he tripped and fell to the blood-soaked carpet. He ended up on his back, looking up at the chaos that surrounded him. People were being torn limb from limb, their flesh gouged by human teeth—children and adults both. Jack was powerless to help any of them—he always was. Every night he was an impotent witness to a thousand deaths. But tonight, the eye bleeders were ignoring him.

And part of him knew why.

Jack's vision went cloudy, and a dull buzzing filled his skull. It was becoming hard to think... to feel. His entire body was numb, and it took only a few minutes more before he lost all sense of himself. His eyes bled, and he got up off the floor to join the shambling mass of infected.

# DAY 103

JACK WOKE UP screaming. He leapt out of bed and started trashing his room, ramming his fists into the television and making them bloody and covered in glass splinters. Then he ripped the bedside cabinets away from the wall and hurled them across the room. He kicked holes in the wall. He pulled doors from their hinges. When security came to apprehend him, they locked him inside the ship's brig and left him there. The tiny square room kept Jack safe from the infection that night, and he sat there in silence until he fell asleep at midnight.

# DAY 104

JACK WOKE UP and smashed up his room again. He spent another night in the brig. It was safe there.

# DAY 198

JACK HAD GIVEN up hope. The last slither of it had died the night Ivor and his family had died in the medical centre. No matter what Jack did, he couldn't stop the infection. He couldn't prevent the passengers from turning into monsters. Nor could he find out what caused it. Even if he knew, it would do no good. It would still kill everybody all the same.

He'd stopped trying to find answers, he'd stopped wondering why this was happening, or whether he was in hell. He dragged himself out of bed at 1400hrs every day and went outside, performing the same rituals over and over. The routine even became comforting in some strange way, and Jack looked forward to the seagull at his window and prepared himself for the boys racing down the Promenade Deck. Predicting the recurring elements of his day put Jack in control, made him master of his own existence. It was all he had.

The sun was out above the pool as it always was. One of Jack's few blessings was the warmth of its rays. It was the one thing that still connected him to the world. Stuck on a cursed ship in the middle of a featureless sea, but he still shared that same sun with the people in Mexico and Japan and England. He was still connected to them in some small way.

Jack decided to take a dip in the water today. He took off his t-shirt and dropped it onto the floor. He stepped in front of a small boy running around the edge of the pool and caught him as he was about to fall. The boy wouldn't know it, but Jack had just saved him from a nasty knee-scrape. He received no thanks for it; however, he never did whenever he saved the boy.

Jack sat on the side of the pool and dangled his legs in the crystalline water. Once he was ready to engulf himself in the water's cold kiss, he slid beneath its surface. The water was frigid enough to make him shudder, but after a few hurried breaststrokes, his body adjusted. The sun beat across his shoulder blades, and the soothing sensation flowed all the way to his toes. Kids swam and played around him, splashing water and throwing inflatable balls to one another. In spite of Jack's usual depression, he found a moment of brief respite. The water was relaxing, and he felt happy—but it was temporary. The pool would lose its charm after a day or two. Everything Jack did became boring. He couldn't even gamble in the casino, for he knew the cards before they were dealt.

Wading over to the edge of the pool, he placed his forearms against the cool cement of the edging. He let his legs float away behind him and closed his eyes, trying to blank his mind, to forget he was trapped in an endless limbo. Was this his punishment? Was it what he deserved for what he'd done—the murders he'd committed? Had his actions damned him to hell? Was he evil?

Jack never thought of his actions as murder—more as justice—but perhaps some celestial judge saw it differently. If there was a God, perhaps He saw murder as a sin regardless of motives. Jack could admit he was a killer, but no way would he ever admit to being an evil man. In the grand scheme of things, he was firmly planted on the side of good—he knew it in his heart. Especially when compared to the countless wicked souls he had spent his lifetime apprehending. He'd spent a majority of his existence trying to help others, trying to make the world a safer place. If this was his reward—damnation—then God could go straight to Hell himself. If He thought He could have done better, then He should try living on this rotten earth for a while. Then God would understand the true shit-hole he had created.

Jack had never been one for contemplation or philosophical thinking, but he turned to it more and more lately as a way of keeping sane. He would ask himself questions to occupy his mind, then obsess over the answers. It was one of the few good ways to pass time. He knew though, that it could only be a matter of time before his mind unraveled from the strain. The loneliness and isolation of his repeating world was destined to drive him mad. He would run out of questions to ask, with no more answers to find.

"Jack?"

The sound of his name shocked him, for nobody ever spoke it anymore. Nobody knew him. He glanced up to find someone standing at the edge of the pool looking at him. The sun shining behind presented the figure as a silhouette, but Jack could still tell who it was. The waitress.

Jack's mouth fell open, and he tried to swallow. He tried to speak but failed. The waitress smiled at him, but she looked weak and weary. She was not wearing the uniform she'd had on when Jack had first met her; she was clothed instead in simple jeans and black t-shirt.

"I think you've been looking for me," she said. "Come with me, Jack. I think I know what is happening."

\* \* \*

Tally's cabin was at the aft of A Deck. When Jack had searched for her, he'd knocked on just about every cabin door on the ship, but most had not opened, and there was no way to tell if people were ignoring him or if the rooms were empty. He'd given up on finding Tally, and as soon as he had, she found him.

Her room was nice, personal, with a wide assortment of chintzy knickknacks adding to its charm. Jack took a seat on the foot of her neatly made bed while she sat on a chair beside the room's cluttered dressing table.

"So what do you know?" Jack asked before she even had time to settle in her seat.

"The day is resetting."

Jack sighed. "I know that! The day keeps repeating over and over."

Tally shook her head. "No, you do not understand. It is not repeating. It is resetting."

"What's the difference?"

"For the day to be repeating, it must first exist, an unchangeable part of our timeline. That is not what is happening. For whatever reason, this day is being wiped clean at midnight and reset to start over."

"But the same things happen every day. Repeating."

Tally looked at Jack as though he was a child. "No. The things that happen on this day are fated to occur. They happen because they are a culmination of the almost infinite events from the days preceding them. What people do tomorrow is a product of what they do today. The world ripples, and those ripples do not change."

Jack tried to understand. He kind of did. People kept acting the same way because they were acting however they would have if the day had just gone on as normal. There were no factors to make them behave any differently, so they didn't. Things only changed when Jack did something to directly influence events.

As if reading his mind, Tally said, "This is why you can change things, Jack. If the day was repeating, so too would you repeat. Your freewill exhibits that the day is being reset, and that you are the only passenger of this ship who can still remember the previous version of events that have been erased. Whoever did this chose you for something."

"And you," Jack added.

Tally shook her head. "No. At first I was like everybody else. I didn't realise what was happening."

"So, what changed? How come you know now?"

"I am Romany. My people have dealt with magic for centuries. We have built up certain… resistances. At first, I was oblivious, the same as everybody else, but the longer the spell was in effect, the more it failed to get through my natural defences. At first, I just felt a little odd, daydreaming about things that hadn't happened—or at least I believed so at the time—but then I realised what was happening. I stayed in my room for many days, trying to make sense of things. On one of those days, I saw you knocking on doors and asking about me. I was frightened, and I hid from you, but I also realised that whatever was going on wasn't just happening to me."

"What is happening?" Jack urged her to tell him because the anticipation was killing him. This woman sitting before him perhaps held the knowledge to end his suffering.

Tally sighed. "I do not know for sure, Jack, but I believe there is a pathwalker aboard this ship."

Jack swallowed a mouthful of saliva and stretched his eyes wide to clear them of their fuzziness. He wanted to make sure he had heard her correctly. "Did you say a pathwalker? What the hell is a pathwalker?"

"A pathwalker is a powerful being. Human, yet… changed. They undergo a ritual at a young age which allows them to see across the many threads of time. They are the true seers of the future and the past, but can also see sideways."

"Sideways?"

"Yes, sideways. Every time you make a decision, Jack, there are a thousand paths you did not follow. Each of those paths plays out in an alternate version of events, with alternate versions of you."

"That sounds a little Movie of the Week to me," Jack said.

Tally did not seem to understand his incredulity. She carried on with her explanation as if she were reading it from a textbook. "Think of time as a piece of string made of many tiny threads. Each time you choose left, another version of you chooses right, and the string is pulled apart into two separate threads. This happens millions of times every second, and the strings eventually become a tangled weave, a tapestry of existence. We call this tapestry the celestial pathways, and a pathwalker can grab ahold of every one of these tiny threads and see the events that transpired there. They can even, sometimes, affect those threads. I think we are seeing an example of that now, although there are consequences."

Jack rubbed his forehead and let out a long, laboured sigh while he tried to absorb everything. It sounded like a bunch of hocus-pocus and new-world superstition, but with what he had been through for the last six months, he had no option but to believe what Tally was telling him. He had to believe in something.

"So, this pathwalker?" he said. "He's evil, right? Like some kind of witch?"

Tally shook her head. "No, Jack. Not at all. Pathwalkers are good. They are protectors of the world. I do not know why one might do this, but it will be for good reason."

Jack couldn't believe what he was hearing. He couldn't agree that anyone responsible for the hell he was in was good. There was just no way. Jack had to find out who this pathwalker was and force him to stop doing whatever it was he was doing. This madness had to stop. Even if it meant he had to kill the son of a bitch.

# DAY 199

JACK HAD GONE back to his room after talking to Tally. He'd needed to think things through. What Tally had told him about pathwalkers and time-threads was a lot to take in for a sane person. This already crazy world had grown to include time-controlling wizards and magic-resistant Romany gypsies—and he'd been selected to play some part in a plan he knew nothing about. Tally hadn't even got around to discussing the virus on board. It had almost seemed like a background event to her.

Jack had thought he was in Hell for the sins he had committed, but now he found himself struggling to believe another version of events. Why had this pathwalker—he felt stupid even thinking the word—picked him over a thousand other passengers? What was so special about Jack?

He'd woken that day at 1400hrs, as always. In some way, he had hoped new knowledge of the situation would have been enough by itself to break the spell.

No such luck.

He'd agreed to meet Tally again at around 16:00. It was now a quarter-to and Jack was still lying on the bed in his cabin, clothed and ready to leave. His depression had lifted at the realisation he now had a companion on board—someone with whom he could share his fate. Not being alone made a huge difference to his world. One of his basic human needs restored.

He got up from the bed and went into the bathroom and glanced in the mirror. Although it had been the best part of a year since he'd boarded the Spirit of Kirkpatrick, it looked like he'd aged a whole decade. It was hardly surprising considering the stress and misery he'd been subjected to, but he was also concerned that he might actually be aging. The day was being reset at midnight each night, but he wasn't. He was living through every day as if they were sequential, his life was ticking away.

Jack left his room and took the elevator up to the Broadway Deck. He would meet Tally by the pool and together they could search the ship for the pathwalker. Hopefully, whoever it was would be shrouded by a sphere of glowing light and wearing a mage's robe.

Tally was already waiting when Jack reached the pool. Once again dressed in casual clothing, she seemed to be hiding out from other members of staff. If they saw her, she'd have to explain why she wasn't at work.

"Hey," he said, walking up to her. "How are you?"

"I am fine, thank you. Are you ready?"

"I guess so. Do you have any idea where to start?"

"No. It could be anyone. Pathwalkers have belonged to every race since the dawn of time. They could be as normal as you and I. My mother taught me stories about them from far and wide."

"Great. Just a thousand or so passengers to check on then."

"Plus three-hundred staff."

Jack raised his eyebrows. "Wouldn't you know if it was a member of staff?"

Tally shrugged. "I've not spoken to most of them. It is a big ship, and we all have our own areas."

"So, where should we start?"

She shrugged. "I suppose we should try to make a plan."

"Okay, is there anything to look for specifically to find a pathwalker?"

"They will be outside of the spell, like us. Have you noticed anybody else not following a pattern?"

Jack stared at his shoes and thought it through before looking back at Tally. "I honestly haven't. You were the first person I realised was like me."

"Okay, so we have nothing. We should just start at the bottom and work our way up."

"You mean at the bottom of the ship?"

"Yes. Let's go down to the Orlop Deck—that is the lowest part of the ship. There is a small amount of cargo on board. Maybe that will give us some clues."

"Cargo? I thought this was a cruise liner."

Tally sighed. "The ship is owned by BR shipping. They take advantage of their cruise itineraries by offering free freight service to their subsidiary companies."

Jack scratched his chin. "BR? BR? Where do I know that name from?"

"Black Remedy. They are the largest commercial entity in the world. I would think they are familiar to everybody. Samuel Raymeady is the richest man in the world."

Jack clicked his fingers. "Yeah, that's it, Black Remedy. Jesus. They have their fingers in the holiday business?"

Tally shrugged. "Looks like it. Now come on. We may feel like we have eternity to find the pathwalker, but we do not."

"I don't understand."

"Enough!" Tally took Jack by the arm and dragged him away from the pool. "No more questions," she said. "We have to get started."

* * *

Tally took them to the bowels of the ship via the elevator. She first had to key in a code on the console that allowed her access to the non-passenger parts of the ship.

The Orlop Deck was stifling, lit by fluorescent strip lighting, and possessing no windows or soft furnishings of any kind. An uncarpeted floor left the metal walkway exposed, and the sound of machinery was constant.

"The cargo hold is aft," Tally said. "This way."

They headed down a walkway towards the back of the ship. There were no doorways on this level, and everything was wide open. Up ahead there were several cargo pallets wrapped in saran wrap and secured to the floor by ropes and buckles. Some of the pallets were stacked ten feet high.

"What is all this stuff?" Jack asked.

"BR often transports medicines from their plant in Portugal to other countries in Europe."

"How do you know so much about Black Remedy?"

"Because I like to know who I work for. Plus, all the staff are aware that the lower hold is used for shipping. It is no secret."

"Then what do you expect to find down here?"

"Evidence of a spell."

Jack frowned. "Huh?"

"You cannot just reset time without having certain things prepared. Somewhere on this ship there is a candle burning. If we find it, we find the person who cast the spell."

Jack glanced around the cargo hold at the various boxes and crates. "We're looking for a candle?" he said. "Why didn't you say so earlier?"

"Because if you saw the candle in question, you would have mentioned it anyway."

"Why?"

"Because the candle will burn with a bright blue flame. It's probably being kept somewhere private and undisturbed—like the cargo hold."

Jack moved between the pallets, prodding at various boxes and crates. Sure enough, they all had printed labels reading: BR PHARMACEUTICALS.

"You think this stuff has anything to do with the virus on board?" he said. "What do you make of what has been happening to people every night?"

Tally hoisted herself up onto a pallet with the agility of a circus performer and scanned the area from an elevated position. "I know nothing of the virus except that it is man-made."

"Why do you think it's been engineered?"

"Because nature does not bring back the dead to kill the living. Only man is wicked enough to create such a thing."

Jack pulled at some of the wrapping around a pallet and attempted to get at the contents inside. "Maybe there's some nasty substance in one of these boxes that got loose. I've read things about Black Remedy being involved in all kinds of dodgy practises and corruption in the past—that's how they got so powerful in the first place. Maybe they're into weapons and chemicals and stuff."

Tally sounded uninterested. "Perhaps. It all sounds like a conspiracy to me. I think, if we find the pathwalker, we will find answers for all our questions."

"You think the virus and the day being reset are related?"

She jumped from the top of the pallet and landed right in front of him. "Of course they are. You think that two unnatural things happening at the same time, in the same place, are mere coincidence?"

Jack saw her point. "I suppose not. Then how are they related?"

"I told you," Tally said. "Pathwalkers are a force of good. They protect the world. And right now, one is trying to protect people from the virus aboard this ship. That much is clear. There must be a way to save all of these passengers. That must be your mission."

Jack grunted. "If this pathwalker is so righteous and helpful, why doesn't he come out and help us. Why is he hiding?"

"It may be against the rules."

"The rules?"

"Yes, the rules." Tally seemed to get impatient with his questions. "For magic to be successful, it must be performed within the realms of certain restrictions. To break those rules would bring about catastrophe, especially when manipulating time itself."

It was sounding too hocus-pocus again for Jack, so he resumed his search of the cargo hold. He had the strange sense he was being watched, but he shook it away as paranoia. Up ahead, was a pallet stacked several feet high with blue, plastic crates. They looked like beer coolers, and when he went over to check the contents, he found no labels or identifying marks at all.

"I'll take a look inside one of these boxes," Jack shouted over to Tally. "They don't look like the others."

"What's in there?"

"Only one way to find out." Jack ran his fingertips over the box's seams but could find no obvious way to open it, so he tipped the crate onto its side and cringed when he felt something shift inside.

"There," Tally said, pointing her finger at the crate. "In the corner."

Jack examined the base and saw that one corner featured a keyhole. As he looked closer, he could see that the cargo pallet had been stacked upside down, and all the crates were positioned with their lids pointing at the floor. He could think of no reason to pack everything upside down, other than to prevent people looking inside.

"We need to get this box open," he said.

"I think you should just step away from there, right now," came a voice Jack did not recognise. "No sudden moves, pardner, understand?"

Jack turned around to see a man standing behind him: medium height, average looking, and rather dumb-sounding when he had spoken—despite the threatening intent of his words. He sounded like one of those drawling cowboys from grainy westerns. And just like a cowboy, he was pointing a revolver at Jack.

"Who are you?" Tally asked, not seeming to notice the firearm in the man's left hand. "What are you doing down here?"

"I'll ask the questions, lady. Why are you snooping around other people's property?"

"I am an employee of the ship. I'm allowed to be here."

"Not here, sweetheart. You need to back away and leave this area well alone."

"This is a staff area," Tally told him. "You are the one who must leave."

The man waggled his revolver at her. "D'you realise I have a gun pointed at your pretty little face, lady? I'm not kidding around."

"Shoot me," she said. "Believe me when I tell you, I'll get over it."

The man seemed confused by the comment and the revolver lowered. Jack tried to take control of the conversation while the man was unsure of himself.

He chose politeness as his opening tactic. "Why do you have a gun, sir? Is this area restricted?"

The cowboy's smile was crooked. "Sir? I think I like the sound of that." He moved the gun closer to Jack's face. "But I'm afraid I'm still gonna have to insist you both mosey on out of here. This is my cargo, and you're trespassing."

Jack wasn't going anywhere. "What the hell are you guarding?"

"None of your business. Now get!"

Tally backed away and Jack followed her. They could force the issue and see where it led, but it would be better to take a step back and re-strategize. The ship's cargo hold was being used to transport something they weren't supposed to know about.

"Where are we going now?" Jack asked Tally as they headed back to the elevator.

"We're going to see the captain," she said. "To tell him there's an armed man aboard his ship."

\* \* \*

Tally used her limited credentials to get herself and Jack inside the ship's Bridge. It was clear by the reaction of the technical staff that a waitress was not welcomed in this area, but her insistence—and her exotic beauty—got her through. After convincing a young radioman that there was an urgent matter which needed to be brought to the captain's attention, she and Jack were finally allowed to wait inside a small office. It was set up like a meeting room, with an oblong table and leather-backed chairs arranged at its centre. Both Tally and Jack took a seat.

After a short wait, a white-uniformed man entered the room and observed them. Each arm of his jacket was emblazoned by four horizontal stripes and an executive loop, while his white-peaked cap featured a small emblem of an anchor on a blue oval background, which itself was encircled by a golden wreath of oak leaves. Jack knew from his days in the forces that this man was the ship's commanding officer.

"I am Captain Marangakis," he said, addressing them with the stern tone of a man who had little time to be wasted. "I understand you wish to inform me of something."

"Yes, sir," Tally said.

The captain remained standing, his back straight. "Well? What is it?"

Tally told him. "There's a man with a gun in the cargo area."

The captain stared at them both for a moment, then he pulled up a chair and sat down. Before he said more, he removed his cap and placed it on the desk. His head was balding. "May I ask what you were doing in my cargo area?"

Jack didn't have an answer that would suffice, so he ignored the question and asked his own. "Did you hear what we said? There is a man with a gun down there. Does that not concern you?"

"That man is allowed to be there. He is a member of BR Shipping's maritime security force. He is here to protect their assets."

Jack spluttered. "What? You're telling me you know that your cruise liner, full of children and families, is being used to transport dangerous cargo?"

"Who said it was dangerous?"

Jack sighed. "You don't pay an armed guard to protect something benign."

The captain bored a hole into Jack with his narrow, brown eyes. "I assure you that the cargo on this ship is of no danger to anyone. It is merely BR policy to protect their possessions."

"Okay," Jack said, willing to play along. "Then tell me, what is being stored down there?"

"Who are you to demand anything of me? This is my ship."

"I'm a police officer. Sergeant Jack Wardsley."

"Well, Mr Wardsley," the captain seemed to make a point not to use the word Sergeant. "We are currently one-hundred and sixty miles off the coast of France, so I regret to inform you that your authority is null and void aboard my ship and equally so when we land in a country that is not your own. In fact, right now, I find you guilty of trespassing. What do you think I should do about that?"

Jack tried to calm things. "I respect your authority as captain of this ship, but something is wrong here. People are sick and getting worse. Speak to Doctor Fortuné. I have concerns it may all be a result of what is being held down in your cargo bay. Black Remedy owns this ship, and they are also one of the world's leading investors in medical research. It worries me that they use their own cruise liners as transporters for pharmaceuticals, and God knows what else. It's unethical."

"That may be," the captain agreed, "but it is their ship, and I am their employee. You, sir, are the only danger here. I'm afraid I must insist that you disembark at Cannes. Until then, you will accompany me down to the holding cells. I cannot have you running around my ship spreading your paranoid delusions. You too, young lady." He nodded to Tally. "Your service aboard this vessel is no longer required."

Jack and Tally both sighed in unison, but neither of them resisted. They would try again tomorrow.

# DAY 200

JACK MET TALLY by the elevators on C Deck. They discussed what to do, and both decided that this time they would forget the subtle approach. It seemed the armed guard in the cargo area had free reign to be there, and probably even license to kill if he deemed it necessary. They would only waste time by trying to be gentle.

"So we have a plan then," Tally stated.

"It should work. Not like we have anything to fear, is it? If we get shot, then we'll try something else tomorrow—or today, or whatever. You know what I mean."

They took the elevator back down to the cargo bay and stepped out onto the walkway. Jack stayed back while Tally headed off towards the cargo area, making a big show of being there: clomping her feet on the metal walkway and whistling. Jack crouched and hugged the walls of the hull, ducking behind the various machines and boxes that littered the metal walkway. When Tally reached the shipment pallets in the cargo area, she made a B-line for the blue, plastic crates. She tugged at one, trying to get it free from the pallet. It was seconds before the cowboy appeared behind her.

Jack put his half of the plan into action and crept up behind the gunman while Tally distracted him by crying and begging for him not to shoot. Jack ran up behind the cowboy and struck him in the back of the head with his fist. Years of combat training meant the blow was a guaranteed knockout, and the victim hit the floor face-first. His revolver skittered across the metal walkway.

The plan had worked. Now it was time to get answers.

\* \* \*

The first question Jack asked the cowboy, once the man had regained consciousness, was what his name was. When he refused to answer, Jack pointed the gun and asked again. "Don't make me lose my temper. What's your name?"

"Caleb Donovan."

Jack raised an eyebrow. "You shitting me? What kind of fruity name is that?" Jack was doing his best bad cop impression, hoping that he could use intimidation and insults while Tally used a softer tactic more suited to her age and beauty.

"My name is Caleb Donovan, and that is all you are getting from me."

Jack slapped the man with the back of his hand, feeling no remorse, for any bruises he caused would disappear at midnight. He knelt and looked the man in the eyes. "Look, Caleb. My friend here can turn your cargo upside down, or you can just tell us what's inside. It seems less messy if you go with the latter option."

The cowboy frowned. "Why do you care anyway? Are you here to steal it?"

"Steal what?" Jack asked. "What the hell have you got here? Did you make everybody on board sick?"

"Sick? What are you talking about?"

Jack slapped the man again, but it seemed to have little effect. Donovan's square jaw was more than capable of absorbing a blow or two. If anything, Jack's throbbing hand was coming off worse.

"Do not play ignorant," Tally said. "Someone has infected the passengers with a virus, and you just so happen to work for a company that specialises in medical research. Not to mention you're holed up down here on your own, with a gun."

"It's my job, missy. I'm paid to be down here with a gun. Ask the captain of the ship."

"We did," Jack admitted. "Doesn't mean I trust you or what you're doing down here. Why do you need to protect the cargo?"

"Why d'you think? Pirates, terrorists, opportunistic passengers like you. The world is a dangerous place, pardner. It needs people like me to keep belongings with their rightful owners. Take this situation for instance. Seems I was right to bring a gun on board."

"Pity you couldn't keep ahold of it," Jack said, waving the revolver in front of him. "But we're no thieves. I just want to know what the hell is happening on board this ship."

The man scrunched his face up in confusion. "Why do you keep saying that? What's wrong with the ship? It's cruising along exactly as it's supposed to be."

Jack looked at Donovan and tried to figure out if the man was lying. There were no telltale signs that suggested he was being deceitful—no twitches or furtive glances—but, with an adequate amount of training, anyone could effectively bend the truth.

"What's in the boxes?" Jack demanded.

Donovan sighed. "Look for yourself. I'd rather that then betray my employers."

"Fair enough. Tally, go check it out."

Tally nodded and headed over to the pallet of blue, plastic crates. She clawed at the cellophane wrapping and wrenched one of the boxes free. It fell to the floor as the weight came loose, too heavy for Tally to handle by herself.

"Be careful," Donovan told her.

"It's locked," Tally said, thumbing the edges of the crate.

"Oh, yeah. I forgot," Jack said. "Come check the guy's pockets."

Tally edged over to Donovan, wary of the man, despite him being subdued. Jack kept the gun sighted at the man's chest the whole time, while Tally located the keys in his breast pocket. She headed back over to the crate with them.

"You sure you wanna do this, pardner?" Donovan asked Jack.

"Why wouldn't I?"

"Because you're gunna stir up a shit storm you don't wanna get caught in."

"I'll take my chances."

"Holy shit!" Tally shouted. "Jack, look at this."

Jack spun around to look at the contents of the crate and was shocked by what he saw. In the moment of distraction, Donovan leapt up and took the gun from Jack. He fired two bullets right into his chest.

# DAY 201

JACK WOKE UP breathless. He'd never been shot before, and the pain had been blinding, yet mercifully brief. Now he was in his bed again, ready to start another version of the same day. Every time he got close to any kind of answer, something bad happened and sent him spiralling back to square one. But it was nothing more than a setback this time. Yet, Tally had said something a couple days ago that worried him. We may feel like we have eternity, but we do not. Jack wondered if his ability to withstand bullets to the chest would eventually end. Maybe next time, he would stop waking up in bed unharmed and would just be dead.

He had to find out what the deal was with Donovan and his cargo. Why was the ship's hold crammed with blue plastic crates full of American Dollars? There had been only a brief second to see what Tally had discovered in the crates before Donovan shot him to death, but Jack calculated that if all the crates on all the pallets were full of money, then there was several million dollars in the cargo hold.

Jack hadn't seen what had become of Tally, because he'd been inconveniently dead, but he assumed Donovan would have dealt with her the same way. She probably woke up screaming in her bed the same way he had. He hoped she was okay.

Jack decided to hang around the pool and wait for Tally. It was the most likely place she would go to find him, and he wanted to make sure he was there if she needed him. After performing his morning ritual of saying hello to the seagull at his window, he got in the shower and took a little longer under the steaming torrent of water than usual. His tired and battered body kept him there. He ran his soapy hands over his shoulders, kneading his trapezius muscles and the back of his neck. The pressure felt good, and he moved his hand along his shoulders and inwards towards his chest.

Shit!

Jack hissed in pain as a dull throb erupted behind his ribs. He examined his naked body. Below his left nipple was a patch of discoloured skin—a deep bruise spreading out in a ragged oval shape. It was where the bullets had entered. His injuries hadn't completely healed. Did that mean he could die? The thought filled him with both fear and excitement. He wanted to die, to be released from his torment, but he also wanted to live—especially now that his investigations were getting somewhere.

He dried himself and got out of the shower, putting clothes on and heading for the Lido Deck by the pool. Once there, he headed for the sun deck on the upper balcony. Although he was still eager to discover more about the cash in the hold, he needed five minutes to himself. Discovering that he could now be hurt changed things—made it necessary to think stuff through more cautiously. He was vulnerable again, and that brought him fear.

Claire was upstairs in her usual spot and Jack took the sun lounger beside her, not bothering to remove the green towel.

"I'd move that," she said. "It's been there all day. Probably pretty funky by now."

Jack smiled at her. "I'm sure it's fine. I'll let you know if I start to itch."

"Okay, but if you get fleas don't pass them on to me."

"I promise." He leant over and offered her his hand. "Jack."

"Claire."

"Good to meet you, Claire. You here with anyone?"

"My boyfriend and his mates."

"His mates? None of yours?"

Claire shifted in her seat. "I don't have many friends. I spend all my time with Conner."

"Your boyfriend?"

She nodded.

"I bet you had friends though. I mean, before you got with him?"

Claire didn't answer, just shrugged.

"Well, listen up, Claire. You seem like a nice girl, so I will give you a little advice. I'm older than you, and a police officer, so I've seen it all. I've seen a lot of nice young girls get isolated from their friends and family by a controlling boyfriend. It always happens gradually—so slowly that the girl doesn't even realise what is happening. My advice to you is to get away while you still can. Find your friends and tell them you're sorry. They'll forgive you. Then tell Conner to go take a hike."

"You don't know what you're talking about," she said, but there was a slither of doubt in her voice.

Jack looked her in the eye. "Am I wrong?"

She was silent for a while, but let out a sigh and nodded. "No, you're not wrong. He's horrible to me. Doesn't let me do anything. But I love him. He's just young and acting tough in front of his mates, you know? He'll change, I know he will."

Jack laughed, but he didn't mean it to be cruel. "You realise how many women have said that very same thing before? And how many have regretted it? You shouldn't have to wait for a man to treat you right. You're a nice girl, Claire. One day you'll see the big difference between men and boys. Not all guys will treat you like Conner does. You're wasting your life with him."

"I-I can't leave him."

"Of course you can."

"No, I can't. I'm... we're..."

Jack was about to respond to Claire, but before he could, Conner appeared. Right on schedule, Jack thought.

The lad tilted his head towards Jack and scowled. "How you doing, mate?"

"I'm good. Claire and I were just in the middle of a conversation."

"The conversation's over, mate."

Jack stared at Conner, not breaking eye contact for a single second. "Why is that?"

"What you mean, why is that? Because I soddin' said so."

"Can't Claire make up her own mind? Is she not meant to have a conversation unless you allow it?"

Conner looked at Jack as though he was a new species of ape. "You crazy or something? I'll mess you up, mate."

"I'd very much like to see you to try."

Claire jumped up off her lounger and rushed in front of Conner. "Honey, just leave it. I don't even know the guy."

"She's right," Jack said. "She doesn't know me at all. But I know you, Conner. You're a sad, pathetic little bully who controls women because you're so scared of them leaving you. The reason you think like that is because you're a piece of shit. No girl would ever stay with you unless you chipped away at her until she was nothing."

Claire fought to restrain Conner, who looked as though he might take off like a rocket. She glanced back over her shoulder at Jack and shook her head at him. "I thought you were a police officer. Why are you causing trouble?"

"Police officer?" Conner grunted. "Come on, baby, let's leave this pig alone. He's messed up in the head, innit. Not worth getting arrested for."

The two teenagers headed down the stairs and disappeared. Jack turned his attention to the elderly lovers kissing against the railing for a few moments and wondered what their story was. Had they been in love for decades, or were they both widowers who'd met each other later in life? Who knew?

Jack lay back in his lounger and smiled. The altercation with Conner had been pointless, but had given him a small sense of satisfaction. It was enough of a break from the usual doom and gloom to re-motivate him towards solving the mystery of the ship. As soon as Tally arrived, he would go back to that cargo hold and make Donovan give him the answers he needed. Until then, he would lie back and enjoy the sun. Because, if Donovan shot him again, it may just be the last bit of sun Jack ever got to see. There was something comforting about that.

* * *

Jack awoke in the dark, alone and shivering. The moist, salted air skimmed across the deck and brushed his face. He often fell asleep on the sun deck, but assumed this time Tally would wake him up. She hadn't turned up.

Maybe Donovan shot her in the head and she's dead—really dead.

Jack prodded at the bruising on his chest and huffed in pain. His gunshot wound was a mere abrasion, but what if Tally had taken a bullet to the brain? Or even if she'd healed, would bruising be enough to stop her waking up?

Jack checked his watch and saw it was after 20:00—almost time for the infected to attack. There were limited areas on board that offered safety, and even those would become overrun eventually. The passenger cabins were the most secure, able to withstand the nightly terrors, mostly. Jack thought about going to his room where there was a bottle of Glen Grant with his name on it. He couldn't risk getting hurt tonight, not after waking up with residual bruising from his previous night's fate.

He stood up and breathed in a deep lungful of sea air. The view from the ship was the familiar unending darkness of a night at sea. If he really was in Hell, it was at night time he felt it most. The world became absent once the sun left.

It would happen soon. Jack needed to hurry. His cabin was two decks below, and the elevator was slow. He raced down the stairway to the pool and headed for the Promenade Deck. Probably less than five minutes now until the attacks began, but Jack was confident he could make it to his room.

He hurried inside the corridor and summoned the elevator from the lower decks.

The elevator rose.

Arrived at Jack's floor.

The doors opened.

And someone pointed a gun in his face.

"Hello, pardner. I was hoping to bump into you again."

Jack's eyes went wide. "Donovan?"

\* \* \*

Donovan escorted Jack to the cargo hold, the gun buried against the small of his back the whole time. If it went off, Jack's spine would be shattered. And it might just stay that way.

Jack stepped out onto the steel walkway and headed left under the directions of his captor. They were heading towards the blue crates and the other pallets belonging to the Black Remedy Corporation. The plastic boxes had been pulled free of their cargo and placed on the floor in parallel lines. They were open, displaying millions of dollars in US currency.

"Beautiful, ain't it?" Donovan said.

"What is it for? Why have you put it all out on display?"

Donovan lowered his gun, although he kept it where they both could see it. "In the interest of openness, Jack. Think you and I both want some answers."

"Okay. You think we can be open without the gun?"

Donovan seemed to think before holstering the gun inside a leather slip on his belt. "Fair enough, but you just behave yourself, you hear? You already know I'm not afraid to use it."

Jack's eyes went wide as something occurred to him—something that should have been obvious the moment Donovan stepped out of the elevator. "You mean you remember-"

"Blowing your ribcage to pieces? Yeah, I remember, all right. Yet, here you are now, all alive and such. Ain't it odd?"

Jack was short of breath. "How... how long have you been reliving the day?"

Donovan headed between two pallets and reached into the shadows behind them. He came back with two folding deck chairs and set them out side by side. They each took a seat. "Let me see now... Guess it must be a good six, seven months now. How 'bout you?"

Jack frowned. "I lost track, but probably about the same. How come I've never seen you before? I mean, up until the last couple of days?"

"I have a job to do, to stay here and keep an eye on all this money. Take my profession very seriously, pardner."

Jack looked around at the bare and desolate space and could barely believe it. "You've just been sitting down here on your own for half a year?"

"That about sums it up. Figured whatever's gone wrong will right itself soon enough. Least I used to think so, until I met you and your lady friend, that is."

"Tally? What did you do to her?"

"Nothing," Donovan looked ready to go for his gun at the merest hint of aggression, so Jack stayed quiet. "After I shot you dead, the girl backed off. We had ourselves a little chat and discovered that we're in the same boat—figuratively and literally. Which is why I'm a little more willing now to... cooperate."

Jack leant forwards. "You mean you'll answer my questions?"

"If you'll answer mine."

"Deal."

Donovan got up from the chair, making Jack flinch, but then stepped away and went over to the same pallets from where he'd gotten the deckchairs. This time, he came back with a bottle of bourbon whisky.

Jack grinned. "I think we may have just gotten off on the right foot."

"You a whisky man, Jack?"

"Scotch usually, but what you have there is close enough."

There were no glasses, so Donovan took a swig and handed over the bottle. Jack took a swig, too, and gasped as the liquid burned his gullet. He glanced at his new companion. "What time do you wake up every day?"

"6AM, same as I have my whole life. It's a sin to waste the day."

"I wake up much later than that. In fact, I wake up eight hours later than that."

Donovan whistled. "I'd expect as much from a listless teenager, but a grown man…? Now that's a crime."

"Well, you could say I had a few problems, even before I came aboard this goddamn ship. That's not important now though."

"I guess not. What do you make of all this, Jackie? Your girl said we were under some kind of spell, that some fella, hiding on board, is pressing the cosmic reset button every night."

"Every night at midnight," Jack added.

Donovan took another swig of the bourbon then cleared his throat. "Well, I don't rightly stay up as late as that. I like to get my head down by ten each night. Sleep makes the man."

Jack chuckled. "Maybe that's why I feel like such a shattered mess."

"You got things on your mind, Jackie?"

Jack took a longer swig from the bourbon and lost his breath for a moment. He gave no answer to the man's question. There was no way he would trust Donovan with the absolute truth just yet. Not until he got answers of his own. "What is all this money for, Donovan?"

"From what I understand, it's a bribe. A harmless, run-of-the-mill payoff."

Jack frowned. "To whom?"

"Tunisian Government."

Jack swallowed and tried to follow. "Why would Black Remedy be sending a load of US currency to North Africa?"

"Because the people there just overthrew their president. There's a new guy in town that's a little more with the times. He has plans to start a new Tunisian health service—much like your National Health Service. Black Remedy wants to ensure that they get the contract to supply said service. Tunisia's currency isn't worth a damn internationally, hence the US cash."

Jack rolled his eyes. "Sounds like this new president is as corrupt as the old one."

Donovan smiled in amusement. "But at least this guy's a corrupt democrat. That's about as good as a country like Tunisia can hope for at the moment."

"So what then," Jack asked, wanting to get the full picture. "You're supposed to deliver the cash to a person?"

"After the ship finishes its itinerary of the Mediterranean, it's heading to Algiers and then on to Tunis, where the cash will be collected at the docks. There're a few pallets of pharmaceuticals as well to act as samples for the new health service, and some other bits and bobs I won't go into."

"So that's it?" Jack said. "All this money, the drugs, and you with a gun, is just down to a bunch of corporate corruption?"

Donovan set the bottle of bourbon on the floor between his legs and leant his elbows on his knees, looking Jack in the eyes. "That's about the gist of it, pardner. Truth be told, I have no more of a clue about what's going on than you do. I've been sitting down here, day after day, thinking this whole thing was about me—supposing I was in a coma or something. Figured I was stuck in some sorta weird dream."

"I wonder why you haven't been affected like everybody else." Jack pondered. "Tally said I was chosen by whoever cast the spell, but what's your role in all this?"

Donovan shrugged. "Now I've met you, Jackie, my best guess would be that whatever Hoodoo this practical joker has been casting doesn't extend to the cargo hold. I mean, why would it? There's not supposed to be anybody down here. My being here is a secret. I figure it takes a lot of effort to cast a spell that messes with time itself, so why stretch it further than you have to?"

"You really think that the cargo deck is unaffected?"

"In fact," said Donovan. "I can pretty much prove it."

"How?"

Donovan picked up the whisky bottle from the floor and sloshed the liquid inside. "Because, Jack, tomorrow morning, when I wake up, this bottle will still be empty, and I'll have to go upstairs and buy another one. The ship's been sailing nowhere for months now, but anything that happens down here stays just the way I leave it."

Jack stared at the half-empty bottle in shock. The more he learned, the weirder it became. If what Donovan was saying was true, then the lower deck of the ship was a sanctuary from the spell. Time existed here as it was supposed to. It didn't make complete sense, but it was another valuable piece of the puzzle. Knowledge was power, and Jack felt he needed to know everything he could to have any chance of getting out of this mess.

"What about the virus?" he asked Donovan. "Black Remedy has to be behind it."

Donovan shrugged. "I know nothing about it, you have my word. Seems kind of counter-intuitive, if you ask me. If the ship is overrun with a lethal biohazard, there won't be much chance of the cargo reaching Tunis, will there? Whoever caused the outbreak is unlikely to have anything to do with Black Remedy."

Jack sighed. "Then I'm out of answers. I was hoping these crates would be full of diseased monkey parts, or phials of glowing green liquid. Would have made things simpler."

"Sorry to disappoint you, Jackie."

Jack waved a hand. "Don't worry about it. I guess I need to go back to the drawing board."

"Perhaps. But not tonight, pardner. Tonight we drink and make merry."

"I don't have time for that."

"Like hell you don't. I've been isolated down here for over six months. You're gunna have a knees-up with me tonight, even if I have to shoot you to keep you here."

Donovan was probably joking about shooting him, but Jack thought the invitation wasn't the worst idea he'd heard lately. It would be nice to take a break for just one night. Upstairs, the passengers would already have torn each other apart. It was too late to help them, not that he'd even planned to.

"Okay," Jack said, picking the bottle of bourbon up off the floor. "What's the first thing you'll do when you get off this horrible bloody ship?"

Donovan grinned at Jack and said, "I'll go get a flu shot."

\* \* \*

"So how long have you worked for Black Remedy?"

"Not long." Donovan's voice was approaching a full-on slur now. "I was a prom-promis... promising young boxer once, if you can believe it. Got hurt pretty bad before I ever got the chance to... belch... to really make it though. I could have been a contender, maybe made a comeback, but my girl was against it. In the end, I did what made her happy." He shook his head and sighed. "Then my girl up and leaves me a year later, and both my parents pass on within the same decade. If it wasn't for shit luck I'd have no luck at all." He took another swig of the bourbon and spoke in a croaky voice. "Anyway, started doing private security when I hit twenty-five-or-so. Been doing it ever since. Black Remedy is just the latest in a long line of gigs. The pay is good, but not as good as if I'd been a professional fighter. Don't that just suck?"

"Yeah, that sucks," Jack admitted. "Still, least you were good at something. My whole life has been the epitome of average—average kid, average teenager, average police officer, and not much else."

Donovan looked at Jack with bleary eyes. "You... you're a cop? That's not average. That's honourable. You p-p-protect people."

Jack shook his head, which made his drunken vision tilt to and fro. "That's American cops you're talking about. British cops spend most of their time dealing with drunks, wife-beaters, and bad drivers. We do nothing to make a real difference. Goddamn justice system protects the criminals more than it does the public. It's become cool to be a thug in the UK."

"Then why... why don't you... why don't you do something about it?"

Jack laughed. "You think it's that easy? I'm just a sergeant. No one listens to me. Anyway, I did do something."

Donovan leant forward. "Oh really? What did you do, Jackie?"

"I killed a bunch of drug-dealing scumbags. Took them out while they were all lying around stoned. One of them even giggled when I slit his throat. Never seen anything like it in my life—not even in the army. Drugs make people so screwed up they laugh at their own murder."

Donovan was looking at Jack with wide, worried eyes. "That's stone cold. You rolled up and killed them all, no kidding? The hell got into you?"

"My partner was shot to death. She was trying to help a family being terrorised by a bunch of yobbos. The leader of the gang was a degenerate named Frankie Walker. He shot my partner in the hospital while she was checking on one of his victims. When I got there, she was lying against the wall in a pool of blood, already dead. Her face was grey, like it was carved in ash. She was a beautiful person, Donovan, and this Frankie snuffed her out like a cigarette butt. He was dead at the scene too—shot by his own brother. His gang remained on the streets though, still intimidating people and acting like they owned the place. I dealt with it. I dealt with them all."

Donovan said nothing. He just looked at Jack. It was the first time Jack had spoken of his actions. To speak freely about such things would have landed him in prison. His superiors had found out what had happened from a not-yet-completely-dead witness at the scene, but they covered it up lest the public condemn the entire service. Most of Jack's colleagues were partly glad that a prolific street gang had been put out of action, and there was little sympathy for the victims, but the men and women Jack once considered friends were now suddenly afraid of him. He became isolated and angry, a loose cannon with nobody to remind him of the rules but himself. The decision to protect Jack by covering up his crime proved to be a mistake. He had gone off the rails even further and was now untouchable by virtue of the secret binding him and his superiors together.

"You must have loved her a lot," Donovan said. "A man doesn't feel that much rage unless he's failed to protect the woman he loves."

"We'd been together a little while but had been hiding it from our colleagues. We were saving enough money to get a house, and then Laura was going to quit the force and have a child with me. I lost everything."

"And someone had to pay?"

"I don't regret it."

"Well, I don't blame you, pardner. Seems that the world gets worse and worse each day. 'Bout time good folks fought back. Still, how the hell did you get away with such a thing?"

"I didn't. I got suspended from the force, under the guise of bereavement—having my partner killed and all—and they stuck me in therapy for six months. Started drinking, stopped looking after myself. After a couple years watching me self-destruct, my bosses sent me on this cruise, to break me out of the emotional tailspin I'd been in since Laura died. Their final gesture of kindness before they discharge me. Tell you the truth, if things ever go back to normal, that's just what I want. I can't do the job anymore. I've seen how little justice there is in the world and can't be a part of a broken system anymore."

"Hey, I hear ya. Ain't no place left that hasn't witnessed the evil of Man. Bad guys all over."

Jack gave Donovan a surprised look. "Yeah, and you're one of those bad guys."

"What's that now?"

"You're delivering bribe money to a corrupt politician."

Donovan seemed to think about it. "Well, yeah, I guess, now you mention it, I am one of the bad guys. Maybe I'll rethink things too if this nonsense ever ends."

Jack snorted. "This nonsense? That's one way to put it."

Donovan swigged the last drop of the whisky and leant back in his chair with a satisfied grin on his face. "Hell, that's the only way to describe it, far as I'm concerned. I've never known anything make less sense in my life."

"You're right," Jack said. "This is all a big load of nonsense. I still need to get to the bottom of it though."

Donovan stood up, disappeared for a moment, and then returned with another bottle of bourbon. "You sure do, but there's no need to rush, pardner. You came on this cruse to relax. So relax."

Jack took another swig and did just that.

# DAY 215

TWO WHOLE WEEKS went by in a daze of whisky-fuelled madness. Jack and Donovan had started their friendship playing cards in the cargo hold, but progressed to full-on hellraising in the ship's various clubs and casinos. Donovan often ended his nights with drunken dalliances involving any women as wasted as he was. Jack would often retire with a bottle of Scotch as his companion.

One night, Donovan confided to Jack that he'd been close to losing his sanity by the time he and Tally had stumbled upon him. Learning he was not alone had changed everything—had made him see the fun that could be had with the situation. Jack was growing concerned with the American's reckless pursuit of distraction, but he could hardly blame him after being cooped up alone for six months. Jack kept reminding himself that anything Donovan did was inconsequential. The day always reset, regardless of what they got up to at night.

Tally had been missing ever since the night Jack took a bullet to the chest. He'd checked her cabin several times and several areas of the ship, but she was nowhere to be found. Whatever she was doing, she clearly did not want company. Jack just hoped that she was okay and would seek him out when she was ready.

It was 5PM, and Jack was in the Voyager's Lounge. It was the quietest drinking venue on the ship; therefore, the least likely place to run into Donovan. Jack had nothing against the over-zealous American—in fact he liked the guy—but he needed a break from the partying for one night. It was time to get his thoughts back in order and focus on the things that mattered. Things like the virus on board that still slaughtered everybody each night.

There was a single person who frequented the Voyager's Lounge that displayed symptoms of the virus, an older gentleman in an evening jacket and spectacles. He was always alone and always reading a magazine. His wet sneezes proceeded constant wipings of his nose. In just a few hours, the man would bleed from his eyes and tear into the flesh of anyone unlucky enough to be within sight of him. But for now, he was just an ordinary man trying to relax on vacation.

It was hard to humanize the eye bleeders once they turned, so irrational and violent were they, but it was important to remember that, prior to their conditions, they were ordinary people—people with families, like Ivor and his girls. Jack was trapped on this boat, forced to relive the day over and over, but so was Ivor. The poor man had to watch his family die every night.

Jack was realising his situation was better than most, which was why he'd decided he would find a way to put a stop to whatever was happening. It was selfish to spend his time drinking with Donovan. Jack still had the benefit of freewill, and it was up to him to end everybody's suffering. Whether the passengers knew it or not, they were relying on Jack to save them.

Joma tended bar as he always did at this time. His shift started late and would continue until the eye bleeders arrived. Jack had never seen whatever fate befell the friendly waiter, but it was safe to assume he died a grisly death like everybody else.

"Hello, Mr Jack," Joma said from behind the beer taps. "I hope that your room is to your liking."

Jack had to think for a minute, then realised that, to Joma's understanding, Jack had entered his cabin for the first time yesterday.

"Yes," Jack replied. "Feels like home already."

"That is very good. Can I get for you a drink?"

"Yes, I think I fancy a pint of lager, please."

Jack handed over his cabin card for the drink to be added to his account, but Joma waved it away. "One free of charge. You give Joma good tip and he looks after you."

Jack couldn't even remember how much he'd given the man now; it was so long ago, but he took his free pint gladly and nodded his thanks.

Joma picked up an empty wine glass and polished it. "There's a bad cold going around today, no?"

"Real bad. Thought no one else had noticed."

"Joma noticed. Many people sick today. Sneezing, coughing, very bad."

"You don't look so hot yourself," Jack commented as he examined Joma's face. "You look exhausted."

Joma seemed embarrassed that the focus of the conversation had turned to him. "Joma is fine, Mr Jack. He just work long hours. Lots to be done, many drinks to be served. It is tiring work."

Jack looked at the man and placed him at a little over forty, which was strange because when they'd first met, he would have placed him at a little under.

"So how long have you worked on the Kirkpatrick, Joma?"

"Almost four month now. Joma work aboard different ship before."

"Why did you change?"

"Changing of scenery."

"I suppose one perk of the job is being able to travel the world."

Joma smiled and seemed to look off into the distance. "That is true, but I miss home very much. The most beautiful places are where people love you. The Mediterranean cannot compare to home. Do you agree?"

Jack sipped from his pint and placed it on the bar. "Perhaps I would have agreed with you once."

"But no longer?"

"Where do you find beauty when nobody loves you?"

Joma thought about it while polishing another glass. "I think you find it in hope, Mr Jack. Hope that one day somebody will love you. I pray you find love, my friend. A man is stronger with love."

"I hope I get the chance one day to see if you're right."

"Joma has no doubt. Another drink?"

Jack glanced at his near-empty pint glass and was shocked he had drunk it so fast. "Yeah, make it a whisky, please. Cheers."

Joma got to work, thrusting a low-baller glass against the base of the optic and pouring the brownish-gold liquid in a measured amount. He handed the glass to Jack and smiled. "Joma have to charge you for that one, my friend. He loses job otherwise."

"No problem." Jack handed over his cabin card. "Say, do you know a girl named Tally? She works the Lido Deck during the day."

Joma raised an eyebrow at him. "You make a friend already? Yes, Joma know Tally. Pretty girl. You like?"

Jack felt his cheeks blush and wondered why he'd had that reaction. "Yes, I like her, but not in that way. I was just wondering where she goes at night."

"Unsure, but some of the day-staff like to sneak off to the Sports Deck at night. It is closed to passengers then, and they like to go have drink together. Perhaps you find her there."

Jack thought back to the last time he had visited the Sports Deck. It hadn't been locked up then. In fact, it had been full of children trapped inside the Perspex enclosure like sardines.

Jack turned back to Joma and asked him a question. "Are you sure the Sports Deck is locked up at night? I'm sure I saw children up there a few months... uh, late last night."

Joma nodded. "They have an under-twelve football match between 20:00 and 21:00, but other than that, it is locked up tight. Too dark for people to be running around outside on deck. Dangerous."

Jack glanced back around at the bespectacled gentleman in the corner who had gone from sniffling to coughing and hacking up phlegm. It would be an hour until the Sports Deck teemed with eye bleeders. If Tally was there, as Joma suggested she might be, it would not be a great time to talk to her. He needed to get back to his cabin for now, where it was safe. He'd visit the Sports Deck earlier tomorrow and try to find Tally, hopefully convince her to help him again.

The thought of seeing Tally sent a shiver through Jack's spine. He wanted to see her. Maybe he would find out what had made her disappear.

# DAY 216

JACK CHECKED THE ship's newsletter that came under his door every day and learned that the Sports Deck was open until 6PM. He decided he would get there an hour before. If what Joma had told him was correct, he'd be asked to leave, and the deck would then remain empty until the children arrived at 8PM.

At the Sports Deck, in the mid-afternoon, people milled about Jack everywhere. Young couples batted tennis balls back and forth while an older generation played bowls on a small green in the corner. Ahead, the enclosed football pitch that would later play host to a monstrous siege. It was a place of fun and hijinks, which made its eventual fate even more tragic.

Jack took a seat on a spectator bench beside the tennis courts and watched a game being contested between two teenage girls. They seemed very competitive and even donned the appropriate athletic skirts and nondescript white panties. If only they knew how little their game meant.

The Mediterranean Sea shone gold beneath the wide rays of the setting sun. Once the sun disappeared, the ship would be surrounded by featureless night. The pleasantness of day always gave way to the horrors of night.

Jack shivered at the thought of the approaching darkness creeping towards the ship, ready to engulf it. He hoped Tally would turn up soon, for there was something about the Sports Deck that sapped him of strength. All of this young life and joyful energy made Jack miss the world. What he now wanted more than anything was to just go back to his old life. He wanted his actions to matter again. He may have become jaded by his impotency as a police officer, but at least there was always the hope he would do some good. But on board this damned ship, his actions were useless, his effect on the world less than a mayfly.

Sitting alone, surrounded by oblivious, happy souls, Jack found his thoughts turning to Laura. He didn't want his mind to go there, but he was powerless to stop it. His memories charged forth, a trainload of grief crashing through his emotional barriers and forcing their way into his consciousness. His partner was thirty when Frankie Walker shot her in the stomach. There had been no need for him to kill her. He did so just for kicks. The decline of young morals in the UK seemed an unstoppable force. They screwed each other indiscriminately in every hole, snorted drugs from A to Z, attacked each other, and robbed old ladies when as young as ten years old. The UK was anarchy. And it was getting worse.

But Laura had always seen the best in people. She believed in the inherent goodness of society and that people would generally make the right decisions if given the chance. It was a naïve outlook, Jack used to think, but he had often envied her. It must have been a great comfort to see the world in such positive colours instead of the bleak, black grime and sodden greys that Jack did.

Jack missed Laura's smile—the one she showed in private when the two of them were alone. But he knew he would never get to see it again, erased from the world by the ills of a sick, decaying society. Laura had died because she'd made the mistake of showing compassion for a husband trying to protect his family. The husband's wife and child had been tortured and stabbed by a local gang. Then the husband murdered one of the thugs in revenge. Laura and Jack were given strict orders to take the husband in—and they had the chance to—but he had begged them for one more night to finish what he'd started. Laura had said yes, and despite his better judgement, Jack had gone along with it. They had let the husband go. He knew it had been crazy. The only reason he went along with it was because he loved Laura. That love had made him weak—not strong, like Joma suggested—and he'd been unable to do his job the way he knew he should. He should have been angry with Laura for that, but it was just who she was—and he could never blame her for that. He wished, more than anything, he could go back to that evening and arrest the husband. No one else would have died that night. Frankie Walker wouldn't have ended up cornered with a gun and Laura wouldn't have been trapped inside a hospital room with him. She'd still be alive. And jack's hands would be clean of blood.

Footsteps behind him.

Jack's eye caught movement to his side and snapped him of his daze. Tally had entered the Sports Deck, copped one look at Jack, then turned back around and tried to leave. She wasn't quick enough though, and Jack caught up with her in the corridor.

He placed a hand on her shoulder and spun her around to face him. "Why have you been hiding from me?"

She shrugged free of his grip and looked angry. "I haven't been hiding from you. I've been coming here every night. You just haven't seen me."

Jack tried to stay calm. "Why have you been coming here instead of coming to see me? I thought we were friends."

Tally laughed, a cruel sound. "We are not friends, Jack. We are just two lost souls floating in the abyss."

"But you were the one that said there was a reason for all this, that there was a way to stop it. We haven't found the pathwalker yet. We can still find a way to end this."

Tally rolled her eyes. "We have not found the pathwalker because he does not wish to be found. Whatever is happening on this ship has nothing to do with me, Jack. I wasn't chosen—you were. The only reason I'm even in this mess is because of my heritage. If I was not Romany, then I would be as ignorant as everybody else. I wish I was."

"Me too," Jack said, "but that's not how life goes, is it? When it rains shit, it's not always up to us whether we have an umbrella."

Tally looked at Jack like she was mad, but then she cracked a smile and shook her head.

Jack grinned too. "See? It's easier to face all this with company—I mean, company who still remembers you in the morning. We shouldn't be alone in this, Tally."

"We'll soon get sick of each other, Jack. Doesn't matter how much I like you, I don't want to spend the next thousand years with you."

"You admit you like me then? Here I was, thinking you were avoiding me."

Tally rubbed both her eyes with the palms of her hands. "God, Jack. I don't know how much more of this I can take. I want it to be over. I want my life back. I have a daughter back home."

Jack's jaw tightened. "Shit, Tally. You never told me that. What's her name?"

The tears came quickly. Jack wrapped his arms around Tally's shoulders and kissed the top of her head. If only there was something he could say.

"Her name is Delilah," she said into his shoulder, "and she is my little angel. I miss her, Jack. My heart is bleeding into my chest and only seeing her face again will heal it. Damn it, I need a drink. Can we go get one?"

Jack agreed. "We'll go to the bar."

Tally shook her head. "No! I can't be around other people at the moment. They remind me of what I've lost. Do you have anything to drink in your cabin?"

Jack chuckled. "Hope you like Scotch."

"I suppose it will do. Long as it will get me drunk."

"Oh, it'll do that all right."

Jack took Tally to his room.

* * *

Half the bottle of Glen Grant had gone, and Jack's vision was bleary. He'd been drinking alcohol most days now, for two weeks at least, but his tolerance never increased. Every night at midnight the day reset, and Jack's constitution reverted to how it was the day he'd first boarded. When you considered the fact he was still aging, it seemed a little unfair.

Tally was as drunk as he was, lying on the bed and staring, transfixed by the television. Toy Story 3 was playing, and a big pink bear was stomping around a playroom like a tyrant while the other toys cowered. Jack wondered if the film would make Tally miss her daughter, so he pressed a button on the remote and switched the channel to something else: an infomercial about Cannes—their ever unreachable destination.

"So are you going to tell me what happened?" he asked her. "Why did you disappear on me?"

Tally rolled onto her side and faced him on the bed. "I needed time alone. Some of the crew go to the Sports Deck for a drink at night, so I thought I would join them, try to forget about things for a while. It worked the first night, and I even had fun. It was just staff members, and none of them were sneezing or coughing. I thought it would be a good place to stay during the attacks. But..."

Jack knew the story already. "At 8PM a bunch of children showed up?"

Tally seemed to recall the memory in vivid detail. Wrinkles appeared across her brow. "Yes. A couple of them were under the weather, so they sat on the side-lines with their parents. A lot of the adults were also ill. I knew then that things would go bad."

"And you were right," Jack said, remembering the trapped children from his own experience on the Sports Deck.

Tally continued. "When the attacks started, some of the children started leaking... leaking blood from their eyes. A couple members of the staff locked up the healthy children in the football enclosure to keep them safe, and without thinking, I ran in after them. It wasn't as safe as I'd hoped." She sobbed. "We were trapped in there for hours, Jack, while mutilated children and their torn-apart families tried to get in at us. There was so much blood up against the glass that, after a while, I couldn't even see out anymore. I could just hear the moans and whining of the infected people. The dead people."

"You think the infected are dead when they attack?" Jack had made a similar summation himself a long time ago—ever since meeting Doctor Fortuné. It was good to hear he wasn't alone in this theory.

"I saw a man with his intestines hanging out. He kept tripping on them as he walked around the deck. There was no way he was alive. The infection kills them, and then they get up again. It is evil, Jack. Whatever it is, and whoever created it, is pure evil. Being with all those children, trapped and scared, while other children—dead children—tried to get at them, it... it broke me. I kept going back, hoping I could do something, but it happens the same way every time. There's no way to stop it. We are in Hell."

Jack looked at her and could see the pain etched across her face. Even if things worked out, neither of them would ever be the same. A part of their souls, their spirits, had been broken.

"We can put a stop to this, Tally. Someone is responsible, and they need to pay. We'll make them pay."

Tally nodded at him. It seemed as if she was finally back on his side. "You still think it has something to do with what is down in the cargo?"

Jack said, "No. Donovan showed me everything. He's as clueless about all this as we are. The cargo is full of money and pharmaceuticals—normal pharmaceuticals. The money is just a payoff to some dodgy Tunisian official. Plain old corruption."

"How can you be so sure he is telling the truth, Jack? He shot you."

Jack shrugged. "I've spent the last two weeks getting to know the guy. He seems on the level."

"Maybe it's just an act."

Jack frowned. "What are you getting at? What happened after Donovan shot me? He said that you two talked about things, so you know he's like us, right? That he keeps repeating the day."

"He told me he was expecting us that second night when he shot you, planned to get rid of you so he could be alone with me. Killing you was okay, he said, because it wouldn't be real—just like what he was planning on doing to me. The bruises would be gone in the morning."

Jack swallowed. "What are you saying?"

Tally looked him in the eyes. "What do you think I am saying?"

Jack felt sick. He had shared drinks with Donovan, night after night, as friends, and the whole time he'd been hiding the fact that he had... that he had...

Jack couldn't even say the word.

He closed his eyes and shook the thought away. It hurt too much to think that his mistake, getting shot by Donovan, had cost Tally so much. Jack being killed was temporary, but what Donovan had done to Tally would stay with her forever. There was no reset button for rape. No wonder she had hid herself away.

Jack held Tally in his arms and they kissed. Neither of them instigated it. It just happened. They kissed until midnight stopped them.

# DAY 217

JACK AWOKE IN a rage, but calmed himself down as memories of kissing Tally soothed him. She was gone now, of course, disappeared with the reset, but somehow he could still feel the warmth of her body next to his.

The alarm clock read 14:07. Jack had wasted almost ten minutes in a fuzzy daze as he thought about Tally, but now that those thoughts had gone, his mind returned to vengeance. Donovan was a savage dog that needed putting down. Jack had dealt with monsters like him before during his career as a police officer, and he should have been able to spot the man's true nature. Instead, he'd spent two weeks making merry with the guy. It made Jack's stomach turn.

He got out of bed and forewent his usual shower. He got dressed and removed the unopened Glen Grant bottle. Then he stormed out of his room towards the elevators.

On his way to the upper decks, Jack could not keep still. He paced the small enclosure of the lift and cursed beneath his breath. He felt unsteady, his body coursing with adrenaline, but he also felt strong and powerful—ready for action.

The elevator doors opened and Jack leapt out. He had only meant to step forward, but his anger made his every move erratic and aggressive. The fury inside of him was like nothing he'd ever felt before. By making Jack trust him, Donovan had made him a part of Tally's torment. He would find the man and kill him. Then, when the day reset, he would kill him again. And then again, and again for as long as this whole thing lasted.

Donovan would spend the rest of his days suffering, as Tally would for what he did to her.

Jack knew Donovan would already be in one of the ship's drinking establishments by now, for his day started at 6AM, not 2PM, like his. Carlo's Casino was the cowboy's favourite hangout. Jack was confident he would find him there. And find him he did.

Donovan was standing at the Blackjack table and seemed pleased to see Jack. He lifted his glass in the air and smiled. "Hey, pardner. How you doing?"

"You son of a bitch!" Jack sprinted across the room and made it over to Donovan before the man even had time to lower his drink. He was unprepared for the blow from the Glen Grant bottle, which cracked his skull right above his left eyebrow. The bottle did not break.

As Donovan fell backwards onto the floor, the small gathering of people inside the casino screamed and backed away to the corners of the room. Jack glared down at Donovan, who seemed shocked and confused, holding out his hands in front of him. "What the... what the hell, pardner? Why would you...?"

*"You will regret the day you ever laid a finger on Tally, you piece of shit."*

Before Donovan had chance to reply, Jack bashed his skull in. The heavy whisky bottle finally broke, and Jack was promptly arrested by security. He spent the rest of the day in the brig—but it was worth it.

Tomorrow, he intended to do the same thing all over again.

# DAY 234

JACK HAD TAKEN care of Donovan a dozen times now. Sometimes he would fail to find him, while other times he would find the cowboy trying to hide out in one of the bars or blending in with the crowd on the sun deck. Whenever Jack spotted Donovan, he attacked with a righteous fury that seemed to grow each time they met. Sometimes Jack would bludgeon the man to death like he had with the Glen Grant bottle. Sometimes he would use a knife. Once, he even threw the man overboard and let him drown. But no matter how many times he killed Donovan, it never made Jack feel any better.

At first Donovan had fought back, but after failing to defend himself for the tenth time, even with his concealed handgun, the man had seemed to resign himself to being murdered. He focused more on hiding from Jack than trying to stop him. But Jack had become an unstoppable menace, unwilling to accept any outcome other than Donovan's murder.

Yet he was tiring of the violence. It left a ragged dent in his soul and clawed at the sickly wound opened years before. Jack had allowed rage to overcome him once before, when Laura had died, and it left him numb inside, broken and weary.

Maybe what he needed more than Donovan's death was answers. Perhaps he needed to understand the monster's motivations if he was to gain closure. He wanted to hear the man beg for his life, repent for his sins, and admit what he'd done.

Jack checked all the ship's bars today, and all the restaurants, but Donovan was nowhere to be found. It was early in the day, so most of the passengers were outside in the sun, which made it easier to search the Kirkpatrick's interior. But after almost two hours of looking, Jack had come up empty. Wherever Donovan was, he wasn't in plain sight.

*Where is he hiding? Where would he feel safest?*

The answer came to Jack and seemed obvious. There was one place where Donovan had got the better of Jack. One place where he knew the layout well enough to have the upper hand...

The cowboy was in the cargo hold.

Jack was standing inside the Beluga, the ship's à la carte eatery—a lavishly decorated room with chandeliers and a wall-mounted swordfish, tables set with black and white linens and sparkling cutlery. It was the final place Jack searched for Donovan, but it was another dead end, leaving him certain he knew where to find Donovan.

He headed for the door, but noticed Ivor and his family sat at a table. Ivor stared into space, straight-backed in his chair. Vicky held Heather in her arms, looking teary. The little girl looked ill, yet not as bad as she would be.

For reasons unknown, Jack took a seat at their table. He wanted to give them reassurance, even if it was empty lies. Fate would be unkind to them, so showing a measure of kindness would not be a bad thing.

"Is she okay?" Jack asked Ivor, nodding towards his little girl.

The old soldier broke away from his thoughts and looked at Jack with heavy eyelids. "Yes, she's fine. Who are you?"

Jack offered his hand in a friendly manner. "My name is Jack Wardsley. I'm a police officer from Birmingham. I saw your daughter and wondered if there was anything you needed."

"We need to take her to the doctor," Vicky said, so focused on Heather that she didn't even bother to look at Jack.

Ivor studied Jack. "What exactly do you want, friend?"

Jack thought back to the night Ivor and his family had been attacked, when Ivor had mentioned something about Vicky turning herself in to the police. Maybe that had something to do with the virus on board. "The police know what you're planning," Jack said. "Running away to Germany isn't the right idea."

Ivor's stern expression dissolved into one of fear. "What... how do you...?"

"I did what I thought was best," Vicky blurted out. "The beast deserved it."

Ivor glared at his wife. "Shut up, woman!"

Jack decided it was imperative to keep Vicky talking—she was the weak link here. If the conversation fell too heavily on Jack, it would become obvious he knew nothing. "Tell me about it, Vicky," he said. "Help me understand."

"God, you even know my name? The jig really is up, isn't it?"

"I'm the only police officer on board, Vicky. Tell me what happened, and I'll decide what I'm going to do."

"If you're with the police," said Ivor, "then the only thing you're planning to do is arrest my wife. Well, you'll have to get through me first, friend."

Jack ignored Ivor's posturing and kept his focus on the man's wife. "Just tell me the story, Vicky. I'm listening."

She sighed in a way that suggested she was preparing for an emotional release. "I'm a nurse at the Alexandria Hospital in Redditch. You know it?"

Redditch was a town outside of his policing area, but its hospital had a bad reputation and was regularly under threat of closure. "I know it."

"Well," Vicky continued. "Most of my shifts are on the ICU ward, where I look after people in critical condition. I've been on that ward for a couple years now, and I'm one of the most senior nurses on the floor."

"Okay." Jack nodded. "Go on."

"A few weeks ago they brought in a guy called Nigel Moot."

"Nigel Moot?" Nigel Moot was a prolific serial killer—the UK's first high-profile murderer since Harold Shipman. The man had raped and killed over two-dozen woman in the UK, and many more throughout Europe via his job as a long-distance lorry driver. The last Jack had heard of him—which was a week before he'd boarded the Spirit of Kirkpatrick—Nigel Moot had died in hospital from a severe knife wound to the stomach. His assailant was unidentified, but it was assumed an unknown survivor of an attack took revenge. One of Nigel's victims.

Vicky told him what he already knew, but he let her go on. "Nigel Moot came into hospital with a burst appendix, unconscious and dying. Inside one of his pockets was a photograph of a mutilated woman. When the Police searched his truck and found a secret compartment full of grisly trophies—women's fingers and other horrible mementoes."

"None of that information was released to the public," Jack said. "How did you find all that out?"

"From the police officer posted outside Nigel's room. He wasn't supposed to tell me anything, but I promised to keep it to myself. I was the one who had found the photograph in his pocket. Anyway, once I learned what that man had done, I felt sick to my stomach, disgusted that my time was being used to keep a monster alive. All the women he had killed, all the lives he had destroyed, and here he was, lying in a hospital bed being pumped full of life saving drugs."

"You killed him." Jack stated, knowing he was right by the look on her face.

Vicky nodded, and tears streamed down her clammy cheeks.

"The beast deserved it," Ivor grunted. "In all my days in the army, I never once had the chance to put a stop to someone as evil as Nigel Moot. My wife is a hero."

"I gave him an overdose of morphine," Vicky admitted. "I wasn't thinking. It was like I was on autopilot, and I couldn't think about anything else except ending that wicked man's life. It was stupid, I know. The morphine is tightly regulated, and I was the only person on shift. It was obvious I did it, but I don't regret it. That monster was going to pull through and live out the rest of his days in some plush prison for celebrity inmates. Just look at that Charles Manson guy in America—he's as happy as Larry. I couldn't allow that."

Jack nodded. He looked at Ivor and could see past the man's blustery exterior to the emotions beyond. He adored his wife and would do anything to protect her and his daughter. This was a good family—a loving and supportive unit. Jack wished their futures held better fortune.

He sighed. "I understand what you did, Vicky, and why you did it. To be honest, I would have done the same thing. Perhaps most people would have, if only they were brave enough."

Ivor grunted. "But regretfully, you will still have to arrest her, correct? You plods are all the same."

"No," Jack said, deciding he would tell them a kind lie. "When the boat docks, I'll allow you to leave. I'll say you evaded me. Although, can I give you some advice?"

Ivor and Vicky both nodded.

"Give yourselves in. The public will understand why you did what you did, and the papers will make you a hero. I'd be surprised if you spent more than a couple years in prison, and when you get out, the magazine deals alone will set you up for life. It'll be better than spending your life on the run. You'll have nothing to worry about, I promise. People will understand."

"Perhaps he's right," Vicky said.

Ivor shook his head. "We've been over this again and again. We'll be fine in Germany."

"Well, it's up to you," Jack told them. "I won't stand in your way."

"Why are you helping us?" Vicky asked him.

"Because I'm guilty too. I've also killed people who deserved it."

Ivor's eyes went wide. "I didn't know that the British police force were in the habit of using lethal force."

"They're not," Jack explained. "I wasn't on duty. My partner was murdered, and I did something about it. I tracked down those responsible and killed them. The first murder was difficult, but it got easier. I even enjoyed it by the end. I wished I could have taken out more of them, to be honest."

"Good God, man. Why are you telling us all this?"

"Because it's the truth, and I'll tell you something else as well: I've never been the same since. So believe me, Vicky, when I tell you I understand what you did and what you are going through. It doesn't get any easier. At least you have your family around you. You'll pull through somehow." Jack wished it were true. He would have liked to see Ivor and his family sail off into the sunset together. But it would never happen.

"Thank you," Vicky said. "That means a lot from a stranger—a policeman, no less."

"Yes," Ivor said. "You're a kind man—in the grand scheme of things, at least. And the things you did... I think most people would understand them, too."

Jack got up from the table. "You all take care now. I wish you luck."

He wore a smile on his face the entire time as he headed out of the room, on his way to commit another murder.

* * *

Jack took the elevator down to the cargo hold and resumed his mission to locate Donovan. Funnily enough, out of all the places he'd encountered the cowboy during the last two weeks, the cargo bay wasn't one of them. In fact, it was about the only place that Jack never found the American. Yet, as he arrived there now, Donovan was standing in plain sight, holding his hands up in surrender.

"Given up hiding now?" Jack asked. "You really are pathetic."

"Just calm down there a second, pardner. You been coming at me like a wild bull with its tail on fire for two weeks now, and you haven't once stopped to tell me why."

Jack stalked him, speaking slowly. "You know why."

"I truly don't, pardner. Truth is, you got me terrified. One night we're drinking together, nice as pie, the next you come at me like a mad man. Killing me over and over, for heck's sake, strange as that sounds."

"I wish that were true," Jack snarled, "but we both know that killing someone on this goddamn ship is impossible."

"You believe that, Jackie? Do you really think that what you're doing isn't plain ol' killing?" He lifted his shirt to show a deep purple bruise where Jack had stuck a knife in. "You think that when you stab me, shoot me, or drown me, I'm okay? You told me a story once about how you let rage overcome you. It didn't turn out so well for you, did it?"

Jack thought about how killing the drug dealers had changed him, how it had sickened his soul. But what he had been doing to Donovan was not the same. The man was a rapist—the lowest form of human being.

"You're wandering down a dark and shadowy path, Jackie. You give in to that rage again, after what it did to you the last time, and there might be no coming back from it. We could be stuck on this ship for all eternity. Do you want to lose yourself to violence? Is that how you want to spend your existence?"

Jack's heart pounded in his chest. His fists clenched of their own accord. "What do you suggest I do, then? You're a sick monster. Should I just forget about it?"

Donovan exhaled. "I'm not the one who's sick here, Jackie. You obviously have something inside your head that's making you do these crazy things, and I, for one, would like to know what it is."

"You know what you did, Donovan. Don't deny it."

Jack was through with talking. He lunged for Donovan, but this time the other man was ready for him. This time the cowboy whipped his pistol from its holster and smashed the grip against the bridge of Jack's nose, breaking it. Jack went blind, his vision exploding in bright colours and white flashes. The pain overwhelmed his entire skull. Blood flowed down the back of his throat and choked him. Donovan attacked again, this time smashing his fist into the centre of Jack's chest and crushing the wind from his lungs. He fell to the floor, blind and breathless.

"Now," Donovan said. "I hope I just made it clear, I can take you on any day of the week if I choose to. You're a capable man, Jack, no doubt—but I'm better, understand?"

Jack said nothing until Donovan prodded him with his toecap and caused the pain in his ribs to reignite. "Okay, okay, I understand."

"Good, because the reason I haven't fought back until now is, firstly, because I was pretty darned surprised when you came at me, but secondly, because I like you, Jackie. You're a buddy, stuck in the same shit puddle as me. The kinder part of me is certain that there's a reasonable explanation for your loopy behaviour, but the more cynical side of me is getting pretty worn out with having to fight you. So can we please have a discussion about what we have going on here between us?"

"You know wha-"

Donovan booted Jack in stomach. "No, Jack! I do not know shit about shit, so enough with that, okay? You sound like a self-righteous asshole every time you shout that at me. I don't know why you're so angry, or what I've done to you, but so help me God, you have about six seconds to tell me."

Jack gasped. "T-Tally."

"What are you talking about?" Donovan asked. "What about Tally?"

"You... you raped her, you sick fuck."

Donovan hopped forward and swung his leg like he was taking a penalty kick. The blow caught Jack under the chin and sent him halfway to oblivion. He barely managed to remain conscious—felt like he was falling asleep.

"How dare you accuse me of such thangs," Donovan shouted. His accent had become thicker than ever. "I ain't hurt a woman my whole entire life. You say those thangs 'bout me again, Jackie, and my violent temper is gunna get the better of me, d'you hear?"

Jack rolled himself onto his side and spat a mouthful of blood onto the metal grating. "You... you... you deny it?"

"Deny it? I'm goddamn telling you that the very notion is offensive to me. I don't know what that broad has been filling your head with, but she left this place as happy as a lamb the night you got, you know, plugged. Still sorry about that, by the way, but I guess we're pretty much even now, the way you been behaving."

Jack stumbled up onto his hands and knees, flinched when Donovan reached out to him, but it was an offer of assistance. Jack took the hand and climbed to his feet.

Donovan nodded to him. "You going to behave now, Jackie?"

Jack saw no option but to agree. "I'll listen to what you have to say, but you best be telling the truth, or so help me..."

Donovan pulled out a couple of chairs from the storage space behind the pallets and helped Jack down onto one. "There's only one liar aboard this ship, pardner, and it ain't you or me."

"You really did a number on me," Jack admitted, wincing in his chair.

Donovan chuckled. "Well, you can't say you never had it coming. I wouldn't worry though. I figure you'll be fine this time tomorrow—'cept a little bruising here and there."

Jack huffed. It hurt his ribs. "Tell me why Tally would say you attacked her if you didn't?"

Donovan shrugged. "Beats me. But think about it, you're a police officer."

"What do you mean?"

"I mean that for every two women who've been attacked, there's a third making false allegations to destroy a man's life out of spite."

Jack thought about it. In his years on the police force he had seen women cry rape before when it wasn't true; although he wasn't about to agree that it was as many as one in three, and what was most maddening about those false claims was how much harder it made things for genuinely abused women to seek justice. Nonetheless, it was true that some people were capable of such lies, but was Tally? Jack saw no sense in it.

"Why would Tally want to accuse you?" he said. "What would she have to gain?"

"Your guess is as good as mine, pardner. Maybe it would be best if we went and asked her."

"I don't know about that. She went into hiding after... after what you allegedly did. I don't want to scare her away again."

"Look, Jack. I don't know what her deal is, but she's up to something. I don't understand what she has to gain by making us enemies, but it obviously factors into some agenda she has. Maybe she's behind this whole time-crap-magic that's been going on. Maybe I was getting close to something she didn't want me to see."

Jack laughed. "What, by getting drunk and gambling? You haven't discovered anything."

"Perhaps you're right, but either way, the only person who knows for sure is her."

Jack thought about it and decided he agreed, with certain conditions. "Okay, I'll go find her and talk to her. But you stay here until we speak again."

Donovan sighed. "She convinced you of lies last time, so what makes you so sure you won't buy the same line of bullshit again?"

"Because I'm a good police officer. If I have reason to suspect someone is lying, then I'll know whether they are. I had no reason to doubt her before, but this time I'll search a little deeper."

"Okay, Jackie. I trust you."

"If I find out she's telling the truth…"

Donovan raised his gun at Jack. "Then you and me will have a problem, which is why I'm hoping you're as good as you say you are at detecting bullshit."

Jack turned around and said nothing.

\* \* \*

Jack hadn't seen Tally since the day she'd told him she'd been raped—the night they had lain together like lovers. Jack was mad at himself for not checking in with her sooner—letting his vendetta against Donovan consume him. He couldn't believe he was in a situation that now involved a rape accusation in addition to a deadly manmade virus and a supernatural time spell. Coming aboard the Kirkpatrick to relax was the single most stressful thing in his life. Irony didn't even begin to describe it.

There were likely two places Tally would be: the Sports Deck, if she were still trying to help the children, or her cabin. It was still early in the day, so Jack was guessing the latter. He had a quick think about where she'd led him on the night he'd visited her room. He remembered it was aft on A Deck. He headed for the elevator and pressed the CALL button. Minutes later, he was on A Deck heading towards Tally's cabin. A maid passed him along the way, smiling and nodding, but other than that, the entire deck lay deserted. He located the cabin he thought was Tally's and knocked on the door. After ten seconds of waiting, he knocked again.

Then somebody knocked on the back of Jack's head and the lights went out.

# DAY 235

AT 1400 JACK did not wake up. Not until 1425 did he finally stir. His head whirled with a faraway throbbing. Whatever had struck him in the back of the head had been enough to knock him out cold for the rest of the day, or had perhaps even killed him. Midnight would have eventually come and started things over again. For the first time, Jack had overslept.

Feet pressed against the carpeted floor, he eased himself upwards. The room tilted, and for a moment he thought it was his vision, but then he realised the ship was rocking. He was usually out in the corridor by now, heading for the Promenade Deck and the two racing little boys.

He went into the bathroom and stared at the mirror. The flesh beneath his eyes was dark, and his pupils were wide. He looked tired and felt it too.

He had fallen for Donovan's bullshit.

After leaving the cargo bay for Tally's cabin, Donovan must have followed him and attacked him. It was a risky move because the man knew that Jack wouldn't stay dead, but he'd obviously decided it was time to fight back. In a way, Jack didn't blame the man, but it now made things very clear—Donovan was one of the bad guys.

That familiar anger rose up in Jack's guts, but he took a deep breath and suppressed it. He turned on the taps and splashed cold water on his face. Barring everything else, Donovan had been correct about one thing: Jack's rage was consuming him. It had destroyed his life once before, and now he was allowing it to control him all over again. Stalking the ship like a madman and committing murder would never have been acceptable to the man Jack used to be—the man who had been in love with Laura. Once upon a time, he had believed in justice and doing things by the book. Now he had become something else.

Something still needed to be done about Donovan, but there had already been too much violence. Jack would have to find another way. A way that meant not losing a part of his soul.

He got dressed and sat down on the end of the bed, staring at the blank television screen and thinking about the virus on board. It was still unclear whether it was the reason for everything that was happening. Was there really a way to stop it? To save everyone from their grisly fate? Jack had tried before, but it had been no good. What was he missing? Why was he stuck here? Who was responsible? There were so many questions that his throbbing skull ached even worse.

As he turned his thoughts to how he would spend his day, Jack decided that all he wanted to do was find Tally. He'd been jumped right outside her room, and it was a possibility that Donovan had hurt her again. Jack needed to make sure she was okay.

But when he tried her cabin again, there was no answer. The next place he searched was the Sports Deck, but that too was lacking Tally's presence. He would try again later, but decided, for now, to visit the pool area and sun deck. Perhaps Tally would be working again, trying to find comfort in her old role.

He ordered a drink from the bar in High Spirits and took it out with him to the lounger beside Claire. They exchanged small talk, as usual, but Jack paid no mind to her today. He was more concerned with keeping a lookout for Tally. Every second she didn't appear made him worry worse.

"You're in a nosey mood," Claire said to him.

Jack looked at her, hearing her words but not absorbing them. "Huh?"

"You keep looking around the ship and staring at people."

"Oh. Yeah, I suppose I do. I'm a... health inspector. I travel on cruise liners to look out for signs of infectious illnesses."

Claire went pale. "What?"

Jack put a hand up. "Oh, don't worry. We're talking Avian Flu at worse, and that wouldn't threaten a healthy young girl like you. Have you seen anyone with cold or flu-like symptoms?"

Claire nodded. "My boyfriend."

Jack kept his voice calm, not wanting to panic the poor girl, but saw he had an opportunity to ask her some important questions. "I'm sure there's no reason to worry, but do you know where your boyfriend might have caught it from? Has he been mixing with anyone else under the weather?"

Claire shook her head. "I don't think so, but then I flew out a day earlier than he did. Him and his mates got drunk and missed the original flight. They had to board in Majorca instead of Barcelona like I did."

That was interesting, thought Jack, because Claire was healthy and Conner was not. They had boarded in separate locations. Conner had boarded the same day as Jack, but Jack himself was perfectly fine. He was close to something, but not quite there. "What about your boyfriend's mates? Are they ill?"

"I think so." Claire looked worried. "They had the sniffles this morning at breakfast. I don't know how bad they are though."

"Like I said, no need to worry, miss. I'm sure it's just a cold virus spreading."

"What if it is something worse? Would I be at risk?"

Jack looked at Claire and wondered why she was so concerned about a cold. "No. There's no reason you would be at risk. Flu viruses are only a danger to the elderly, the very young, or-"

"Pregnant women," Claire answered for him.

It all made sense. That was the reason Claire put up with the way Conner treated her. He was the father of her baby.

Jack sighed. He'd seen so many young lives wasted by unplanned pregnancies. A baby was a wonderful thing, but uneducated, jobless teenagers were just adding to the cycle of benefit-supported, ambitionless families that were nothing but a drain on society. Not all were like that, of course, but many were.

"How far along are you?" he asked.

"A few weeks, I think. I haven't told Conner yet. I was planning on doing it this week—tomorrow at the captain's reception probably. We're getting dressed up."

Jack smiled, hoping that one day 'tomorrow' would actually arrive, and that Claire would get to put on her dress. "Well, I hope he takes the news well and that you're very happy together. In the meantime, please don't worry. There is a very good doctor on board, and I have no reason to believe there is anything to worry about." He wished it were the truth.

Right then, Conner's cue to arrive came, and the young couple had their predictable conversation about hotdogs. Jack chose not to get involved today, but was disappointed not to learn more about how Conner caught his flu. The answer was lurking there somewhere, right beneath the surface, like a blackhead, but there hadn't been enough time to squeeze it free.

And Tally still had not appeared.

Jack decided the only other person with possible answers was Donovan. It was time to pay another visit to the cargo hold.

\* \* \*

The cargo bay lay deserted, and Donovan was nowhere to be seen. The pallets and crates were undisturbed. Jack called out and got no answer. He crept around the space, aware Donovan was dangerous and in possession of a firearm.

"I'm done with this, Donovan. Whatever your deal is, I'm ready to put a pin in it for now. When everything goes back to normal, then you and I will have a different conversation. Right now though, all I want is answers. I need to find Tally."

There was still nothing but silence. Jack headed further into the cargo area, looking left and right between boxes of pharmaceuticals and the blue crates of cash. Towards the back of the area were thick metal cases that he'd not noticed before, each the size of a footlocker. Behind them, something else lay on the floor, sticking out into view by just a few inches. Jack took slow steps towards the mystery object, ready to throw a punch at the first sign of a threat.

As he got closer, it became clear what he was looking at. On the floor, sticking out from behind the crates was...

A foot.

Jack found Donovan lying on the floor, covered in blood so thick it had congealed against the metal grating beneath him. The blood was old, his body stiff. The cowboy had been dead for a while. Jack knew enough about rigor mortis to deduce that Donovan had been murdered shortly after speaking with him yesterday. He had not reset at midnight. He wasn't coming back. It also meant that Donovan was not the one who had attacked Jack from behind. Now, more than ever, Jack wanted to speak with Tally.

She had some explaining to do.

# DAY 236

JACK GOT OUT of bed and made a mental checklist of the things he needed to do. Finding Tally was number one. Finding out who the pathwalker was came a close second. Stopping the virus was number three and underlined twice.

There was a knock at the door.

Jack frowned. No one ever knocked on his door.

As the only one left who could exercise freewill, it had to be Tally.

Jack opened the door.

Two large Filipino gentlemen stood there wearing the bright red waist jackets of Security. Jack didn't understand what had brought them there. What had changed?

"Yes," Jack said. "Can I help you?"

"Could you come with us, please, sir?" It wasn't a question; it was an order.

Jack closed the door slightly, bracing his foot behind it to keep it still. "I'm sorry? What is this about?"

The man on the left, identical to his colleague in every way except for a wispy black beard, answered the question. "We've received reports you assaulted a member of staff during the early hours of this morning. We need you to come and answer some questions, please."

Jack balked. "That's impossible. Whom am I supposed to have hurt?"

"Please, sir, if you could just cooperate."

"Cooperate, my arse. I haven't done anything."

The two men tried to barge through into Jack's cabin, but he held the door firm with his foot. The man on the right reached out to grab him but received a punch in the face for his efforts. Jack had been hoping to move past the violence of the past couple of weeks, but it didn't look like he was going to get the chance. He threw an overhand right at the remaining security guard and sent him to the floor to join his partner.

Then he ran—where the hell to, he had no clue. He was in the middle of the Mediterranean Sea, and there was nowhere he could go free of security's reach. There was a chance he could take them all down, but that was only if the team of guards was small. For all Jack knew, there could be a hundred members of security.

He took the elevator up to the Broadway Deck and hurried through the jewellery store and onto the balcony of the theatre in the room beyond. A couple sat drinking at the bar, but nobody else was around. Jack considered sitting down in the corner and lying low, but it was too out in the open to remain undetected. He was at a total loss and close to panic. As a police officer, he was far happier being the pursuer than the pursued.

Who had accused him of assault?

The answer dawned on Jack. There was just one person who could have accused him, someone with a habit for making false allegations.

What the hell was Tally playing at?

Jack heard concerned voices coming from outside of the lounge's main doors and decided it was time to get moving again. He headed out the rear exit and entered the Lido Deck, knowing it would lead out past the 24-hour restaurant and out to the pool area. Once he got there, he would run out of ship and there'd be no place left to run.

As it turned out, Jack wasn't even able to get that far. Spread out throughout the pool area was half-a-dozen security guards. They spotted Jack the moment he stepped out into the sunlight and came at him in unison. Jack held his hands up. At least by allowing himself to face charges, he would get the full lowdown on what he'd been accused of. Hopefully, he would also learn who had accused him.

He already had a good idea.

* * *

Security took Jack down to the brig. He'd been there before. Only this time they placed him in a small interview room instead of a cell. Walking in to meet him was Captain Marangakis. The man did not look happy.

"Captain," Jack acknowledged with a small nod.

Marangakis did not take a seat at the table, but stood behind one of the chairs opposite. The man liked to remain in positions of authority, always looking down. "Are you Mr Jack Wardsley?"

"I am."

"I've been informed that you've been accused of some rather despicable behaviour aboard my ship."

Jack leant forward across the desk. "I haven't hurt anyone. Whoever has told you otherwise is a liar."

Marangakis took a seat, yanking back a chair and dropping himself down with such force that it must have hurt. "The accusation has been made by a member of my crew. I see no reason she would lie."

"It's a she, then?"

"I'm sure you know very well. You'll be placed in the brig and handed over to the French authorities as soon as we make port."

Jack laughed. "And when will that be? I'd love to know."

The captain seemed confused, which was hardly surprising. "We'll be there in a little over twelve hours. I'd be in no hurry if I were you."

"We'll see," Jack said. "Do you want to show me to my room?"

The captain nodded to a guard standing by the door. The burly man went to take Jack by the arm.

"There's no need to get grabby," he said. "I'll play nice."

He accompanied the guard to the cell next door and allowed himself to be locked inside. It was the safest place to be, anyway. Once the infected became violent, they would wreak havoc on every area of the ship, but they wouldn't be able to get inside the brig. After what had happened to Donovan, Jack worried the spell was wearing off, and if the infected were to rip him apart, he might not get put back together again. Despite how much his life sucked, he didn't want to die when he was so close to answers.

The guard left Jack to sit and contemplate his fate. His previous life of walking the streets as a policeman by day and drinking himself into a stupor by night, now seemed like a distant memory—a fuzzy recollection of a vivid dream. It would once have seemed impossible to think it, but Jack was starting to miss the life he had all but lost. Given the chance, he would make more of it then he had. Perhaps that was something positive to come out of this hell.

Jack lay down on the room's uncomfortable cot and closed his eyes.

He awoke a few hours later to the sound of screams and chaos—the noise of passengers being torn apart. The eye bleeders were doing their thing, as punctual as ever. Jack closed his eyes and went back to sleep.

# DAY 237

SECURITY TOOK JACK away again citing the same allegation.

# DAY 245

FOR OVER A week, the ship's guards arrested Jack, and every day he went with them peacefully. His intention was to see how long Tally—if she were in fact responsible— would keep things up. It appeared, however, that she was content to have him detained indefinitely. For some reason, she wanted his movements aboard the ship restricted.

But why?

# DAY 246

JACK GOT OUT of bed and hurried to get dressed. He selected jeans and a white t-shirt from deep within his luggage, along with a baseball cap. The change of clothing might allow him to move undetected by whoever was making accusations about him.

Tally.

He slipped on his trainers and rushed out of his cabin. It had been a matter of minutes since he'd awoken, and it was fast enough to get out of there before the security goons came. How long he could evade them, he did not know, but hopefully he had some time to find Tally and ask her some important questions.

He took the elevator down to the cargo bay, intending to make sure that Donovan was truly dead, but also planning to give the area a more thorough search to see if he could find anything helpful.

The cloying smell crept over him fingering at his nostrils. The odour was death. Jack had come across it many times before, mostly at the homes of lonely pensioners left to perish in their ice-cold flats. The smell of a corpse settling into the fabric of its surroundings.

Donovan still lay dead at the back of the cargo area and had now started to decompose. His flesh was waxy and mottled, and his lips had fallen away from his gums, leaving behind a sneer. The stink of him was putrescence mixed with faeces, and it made Jack's eyes water. He stepped over the body and examined the metal walkway beyond. There was nothing noteworthy he could see, but from the way Donovan's body was angled, it seemed that he had been doing something with one of the metal footlockers. When Jack tried to open the nearest one, he found that it was locked, so he searched Donovan's pockets, cringing at the gelatinous flesh beneath his clothing, and found a set of keys in the man's breast pocket.

Jack tried the keys one after another until he found one that fitted the nearest footlocker. The lid was heavy, and he had to use both hands to lift it up. Once it was open, Jack couldn't believe his eyes.

The crate was full of grenades, packed into a bed of foam. They looked like standard NATO-issue HE grenades, and when Jack checked the other footlockers, he found that they too were full of explosives, and in several cases, assault rifles and side arms.

Regardless of whether Donovan was a bad person, or just a man doing his job, nothing good ever came from giving people guns. If these weapons were to reach Tunisia, they would most certainly result in people's deaths.

But did the guns have anything to do with the virus?

Jack's head ached again. It was time for a drink. Time to think things through.

\* \* \*

Jack visited the Voyager's Lounge. Security was searching everywhere for him, and out of all the places on board, this was among the quietest. So far Jack's low-key disguise had kept him undetected. He'd even walked right past a guard on the Promenade Deck. It was likely that his accuser had described the clothing Jack usually wore—red t-shirt and khaki shorts—and not the clothes he had chosen to wear today.

Jack had been in the Voyager's Lounge for two hours and had downed enough whisky to make his body warm and content. He had made good use of the peace and calm, to think about what his next move was, and somehow the whisky helped. It was clear that the only person who had answers was the elusive pathwalker, but Jack still had no idea who it was—or even what it was—but he was going to make it his main priority from now on. It was something easier said than done though, especially with security on his back each day. There was even a chance that Tally had made up the whole story about pathwalkers just to mess with him.

Joma turned up for his shift, signifying that evening had arrived. Jack went up to order another drink, and thankfully, it didn't seem the friendly bartender knew Jack was wanted for arrest.

"What can Joma get you, sir?"

"I think I fancy a pint, please."

This time Joma didn't offer to pour the drink on the house. He didn't recognise Jack with the baseball cap on. He stepped in front of the lager tap and poured the frothy draught into a spotless pint glass. It was then that Jack noticed something a little weird.

"What happened to your hand, Joma?"

Joma looked down at the wound on his hand and tried to dismiss it as nothing. "Joma burn himself in kitchen."

Jack looked closer. "Looks bad. Is that... is that wax?"

"No, is just cream for burn, Mr Jack."

The wound on Joma's hand was red-raw mixed with a spotty patch of gleaming white substance. It looked like a burn caused by molten wax. Jack stared at Joma and noticed something else: the man had aged at least ten years since the day they'd first met. Joma was no longer around forty, he looked over fifty. And when he had called him 'Mr Jack' he made it clear he remembered Jack—so why no offer of a free pint this time?

Jack's eyes went wide. "You're the pathwalker."

Joma seemed struck by an invisible blow. It seemed like an appropriate reaction for someone who had just had their cover blown.

He nodded at Jack and seemed defeated. "I think we should go somewhere and talk."

"No shit," Jack said.

\* \* \*

In a back room behind the Voyager Lounge bar, Jack took a seat in stunned silence on a small leather sofa. Joma tipped away the pint he'd poured Jack and got him something stronger.

He handed over the new, smaller glass and took a seat on the couch beside Jack. "You're a whisky man, right?"

"You should know by now; you've served me enough times."

Joma shrugged. "You haven't been by for a while."

"What's going on?" Jack asked, cutting straight to the point.

"I think you know," was Joma's reply, no longer speaking in the third-person.

"I haven't got a clue about anything. All I know is that some kind of flu gets loose on board every night and kills everyone. Every single night, over and over and over again. Oh, yeah, and not to forget that there's a small arsenal of weapons in the cargo bay, and someone keeps accusing me of rape—most likely someone who I thought was my friend."

Joma smiled; he seemed to find Jack's frustrations amusing. He raised one palm as if wanting to summon calm upon them both. "I apologise for the turmoil I have brought down on you, Jack, but I assure you it was very necessary. It was only meant to be you who was conscious of the true reality, but there is a gypsy on board I did not know about."

"You mean Tally?"

"Usually I can sense her kind, but she is not an avid follower of her own ancestry—it made her spiritual aura... diluted. If she was a regular practitioner of the magiks then I would have sensed her immediately."

Jack frowned. "Is Tally some sort of witch?"

"No, no. She is just from a people blessed with a natural resistance to magic. Her ancestors were probably close to, what you call, witches, but their traditions are all but lost. I have come across very few Romany who remember the old ways."

## Sea Sick 141

Jack rubbed at his forehead and sighed. Things were getting into mumbo jumbo territory again, and he didn't want his natural cynicism to kick in and cloud his ability to listen.

"What about Donovan?" he asked.

"You mean the American man running around the ship like a drunken cowboy?"

"Yeah, until somebody murdered him."

Joma's eyes narrowed, and his eyebrows lowered.

"You didn't know?" said Jack. "I found him dead yesterday in the cargo hold."

Joma nodded as if something had clicked into place. "The lower deck of the ship was outside the range of my spell. The hull of the ship is stuck in time, but the cargo area within is a vacuum where time exists as normal. There was not supposed to be anyone down there, but it would appear this... Donovan... was an unfortunate stowaway."

"He was transporting weapons and cash to Tunisia to bribe the Government on behalf of Black Remedy."

Joma shrugged. "Such things do not surprise nor concern me. They are inconsequential in the grand scheme of things. What is more worrying is that somebody killed this man in the hold. The only possible suspect is-"

"Tally. I've already started to come to terms with that."

"It could be no one else. If there were another on board outside of the spell, I would know of it. Other than you, she is the only one."

Jack sipped his whisky and looked down at the carpet. He still couldn't fathom why Tally would murder Donovan. He couldn't imagine the petite, beautiful girl committing such a brutal crime and understood no reason why she would.

"Why is she doing this, Joma? Killing Donovan and trying to set me up so I have to go into hiding? I don't see what she has to gain."

"I see many things, Jack, but I cannot see a person's motivations for what they do. Perhaps she seeks to stop you from succeeding in your task."

"Task? What task? If I am here for a reason, I would like to know it. Why you didn't just come find me on day one and tell me."

"That would have been against the rules. A person cursed with the ability to see across the pathways is forbidden from taking direct action to change future events. I must let them play out, but you are not bound by those same rules. You can change things, Jack."

"You're saying you can't get involved, but you can stop time?"

"Not stopping time-"

"Yeah, yeah, resetting it."

"By resetting the day, I am not directly altering events. I am just allowing the possibility for them to play out differently. You are the variable that will decide where the future will lead."

Jack stood up and stretched his legs. The back room was tiny and featured only a sofa and side table, so he walked up to the wall and rested his forehead against it. "Why me?"

"Because you're alone."

Jack turned back around. "What?"

"If you had a family on board, you would not be willing to do the things you have done to find answers. You would have focused only on their safety. Over time, you would have become shattered by their inability to break free of the spell."

"So the reason I'm in this hell is because my life was already a tragic mess?"

"In a way, yes, but I also sensed that you were a protector—someone who values human life."

"Shows what you know. I killed a bunch of people before I came aboard this ship."

"I understand this, Jack. When a man takes a life, it colours his soul. I saw death on you the moment you boarded. Did they deserve it?"

Jack didn't hesitate. "Yes."

"Then that proves you are a man willing to do what is necessary, and what is right. My assessment of you was correct from the very beginning."

"What am I supposed to do?"

Joma stood up and walked over to Jack and placed a hand on his shoulder. "Save the world, my friend. That is what you are supposed to do. How, exactly, I do not know, but once you find a way, all will become clear."

Jack was about to ask what that meant when a body came crashing into the room. It was another waiter. The terrified man was bloody and wounded—a wide gash running down the side of his neck. He tried to speak but could only manage to gargle on his own fluids before falling to the floor, dead.

"Shit." Jack looked at his watch and saw it was 20:24. The infected had turned.

Joma looked down at his dead colleague and shook his head. "We need to get somewhere safe. I didn't realise we'd been talking for so long. I should have locked the door."

Jack looked at the splintered frame of the flimsy door. "I'm not sure it would have made much of a difference. We will have to go out through the bar area." He peered out through the gap in the doorway and saw what he didn't want to. "Damn. There are a couple of eye bleeders out there."

"I can't go out there," Joma said.

"You're going to have to. If we stay in here, they'll get in. Plus, this dead waiter on the floor will be back on his feet soon. I've seen it happen before."

"You need to get them out of the lounge, Jack, and barricade the doors."

"It will be easier if we just run."

"I can't take the risk, Jack. I can't."

Jack pushed the broken door as closed as he could get it, then looked across the small room at Joma. "Why not? Why can't you leave?"

"Because if I die the spell is broken."

Jack's eyes narrowed. "Then you want to be careful I don't bloody kill you. There's nothing I want more than for this goddamn day to end."

"If I die, then this is exactly how the day will end. Everyone on board will become infected. And then it will get a lot worse. I've seen it, Jack. That's what this whole thing is about. If I die tonight, the spell will be broken, and there will be no hope left at all."

No time for Jack to ask questions. One of the infected in the lounge had already spotted him peering out from the doorway and was coming over. It was an overweight man with a torn belly hanging out of his shirt like raw hamburger meat. He sprinted for Jack as soon as he rounded the bar.

Jack braced his back against the broken door and fought to keep it closed. He looked at Joma for answers. "What the hell should I do?"

"Maybe they'll go away if we keep them out of this room."

"Are you serious?"

The infected man behind the door shrieked like an animal, and Jack's body jolted as the weight against the door increased. The other infected passenger in the room had joined the fat man's efforts. Jack wouldn't be able to hold the door for much longer. Joma ran up to help him brace it, but it was awkward for them both to find space and leverage.

"This won't work," he said. "They'll be in here as soon as we start to tire."

"Perhaps they will get tired first," Joma suggested.

"Wake up. They're not like us. I think they can just keep going until something tears them apart."

The conversation became irrelevant when the dead waiter in the middle of the floor twitched. His fingers clawed at the carpet, and a low moan escaped his lips. Jack's skin tightened as he realised they were about to be surrounded by the infected on both sides of the door.

"Your colleague will be on his feet any minute, Joma. We need to deal with him right now."

"You do it," Joma said in a voice so thick it sounded as though he was on the verge of puking. "I'll hold the door."

"You sure you can hold it?"

Joma nodded.

Jack moved away from the door, expecting the two infected people to come crashing through the moment he did so. Fortunately, Joma was able to hold it, allowing Jack to move over to the dead waiter who was clutching at the floor in a clumsy attempt to get to his feet. Blood dripped from the man's eyes and merged with the dye of the carpet fibres. Jack did the only thing he could think of: he raised his foot and brought it down as hard as he could on the waiter's head. The blow was met with a wet thud, but it wasn't enough to do the job, so Jack stamped again, harder, crushing the infected man's skull against the floor.

Then he stamped again.

And again.

The waiter's skull was a pulped mess against the carpet and left Jack feeling sick. Stamping on a person's head was something he never thought he'd ever do.

He turned around to face Joma and realised that the man was about to lose his struggle to keep the door closed. He stumbled away as the door flew open and the two infected passengers piled in.

Jack shoved Joma aside and met the two dead men head on, planting an open-palmed strike against the overweight one. The blow was enough to send the man staggering backwards, colliding with his mate. Jack already knew hand-to-hand didn't work against the infected, but it could at least get them out of the way.

"Joma, stand behind me. When I move, you follow. Understood?"

Joma scuttled behind Jack and stood an inch off his heels. "Understood, Jack."

"Okay. When these two clowns get close enough, I will try to shove them aside. Then we run for it."

Jack made himself rigid, ready to strike like a cobra. The two infected recovered from their disorientation and came at him again. Jack sidestepped them both and shoved out with his arms. Their momentum took them over Jack's outstretched leg, and they clattered to the ground in a heap.

"Run!"

They bolted back into the lounge, which was now empty. The reception area beyond was not. There were almost a dozen infected passengers out in the hallways. They had not yet noticed Jack or Joma standing nearby.

That all changed when the overweight passenger came stumbling out of the lounge's office and let out an animalistic shriek. The noise alerted the others outside, and all at once they turned to look into the lounge area.

"Damn it!" Jack rushed over to the double doors and shoved them closed. A dozen bodies threw themselves against the wood and rabid fingernails tried to claw a way through. Jack turned the lock and put his back to the door, but an arm came smashing through one of the windows and grabbed a hold of his collar. It was sudden and unexpected. Jack had been unprepared to resist. His face was seized by groping fingers and he could smell the sweet, putrid tang of open wounds and bleeding flesh. From behind him, Joma cried out as the overweight man and his companion stalked him around the lounge. Jack needed to get free, or everything he was fighting for would be for nothing.

He grabbed at the errant hand on his collar and yanked it away with a twisting snap! The fingers became tangled in his shirt and kept ahold of him, so he braced his feet against the door and kicked out hard. His t-shirt tore, and he went flying backwards, landing on his hip. The double doors seemed to hold out on their own, despite the frenzied arms poking through the broken window, so Jack scrambled to his feet just in time to save Joma from being tackled to the ground. The overweight man had gotten ahold of him and was struggling to take a bite. The back and forth tussle sent both men off balance.

Jack shoved the overweight man just as Joma was about to tumble over. He pummelled his fists into the man's pudgy face, not because he had any hope of incapacitating him, but because it would at least keep the man down.

"Joma, find me a weapon," he shouted. "Something solid."

After a moment of shocked inactivity, Joma got moving, leaving Jack to deal with the overweight man on the floor by himself. Along with the blood spewing forth from the man's eyes, Jack's barrage of punches had left his face a crimson mask. He was still snarling, though, ready to bite.

Jack was so consumed with keeping his current opponent down that he did not see the other infected passenger coming up on his flank. The man leapt onto Jack's back and instantly began biting and tearing at the back of his neck. Jack screamed out as a chunk of flesh come away from the bone. He shot to his feet with the passenger still clinging to his back. The overweight man rose to his feet, and Jack knew there was no way he could defend himself against both of them.

Suddenly, the weight removed itself from Jack's back, and he spun around to find Joma standing over the body of the infected passenger with a heavy, glass ashtray. One corner of it was covered with blood and matted hair. Jack snatched it away from Joma and turned to the overweight man, who was now on his feet. He brought the ashtray down on the man's head, and no other blows were necessary.

"Okay," Jack said, panting and moaning. "Let's barricade ourselves back inside the office. We have to make it until midnight."

\* \* \*

The infected tried their best to get in, but with the sofa pushed up in front of the office door and several bar tables placed on either side of it, Jack and Joma were relatively safe. Safe enough that Jack had relaxed sufficiently to polish off almost a quarter bottle of whisky. The fuzziness in the bottom of his gut was pleasant and almost made him forget the horror on the other side of the door. The bite on his neck had stopped bleeding and was now just tacky and moist. It throbbed in time with his heartbeat. He didn't have long.

"You need to end this," Joma said, flinching as something unseen tipped over in the lounge. "Time is running out."

Jack took another swig of liquor. "You still haven't told me what it is I'm supposed to do. Is it still against the rules now that your cover is blown?"

"No," Joma said. "You found me, which makes anything I say to you a consequence of your actions, not mine. It is now within the rules that I tell you what you need to know."

"So tell me already!" Jack almost shouted it. "I'm tired, Joma, so goddamn tired of this shit."

Joma rubbed at his face and seemed to have yet more wrinkles. "This virus.... It's not just a danger to the passengers on this ship. It will wipe out the entire world."

"You're shitting me." Jack gulped the whisky down to halfway and let out a long sigh. "And you know this how?"

"I saw it, Jack. People like me, those that can see the pathways, have dreams. These dreams show us glimpses of the future—especially tragic events. We see death on a grand scale. A person's death causes a small pulse in the fabric of existence, but when many people die at once, it creates a ripple that travels in all directions—including backwards. When one of these ripples travels backwards, it can reach some people through their dreams. I dreamt of this ship, Jack. I dreamt of the virus. I saw the end."

"So this virus turns into... what? An epidemic?"

"More like a global pandemic. It will wipe the earth clean of life in less than a year. The world will fall apart. It will be hell on earth."

"How does it happen?"

"The ship will dock in Cannes tomorrow, and from there, the virus will spread throughout Europe and into Asia, reaching farther afield through national airports and contaminated food shipments. Once the Spirit of Kirkpatrick hits the mainland, the virus will become unstoppable."

Jack swallowed and found his throat unbearably dry. "I don't get it. Who would want to unleash something like this?"

"I don't know, Jack. When I had the dream, I caught short flashes of the man responsible, but whenever I tried to focus, I kept getting images of a... of a doll's face. All I know for sure is that if you do not stop this virus from reaching the shores of France, everyone is doomed."

Jack wobbled. The throbbing of his neck wound had progressed to a full-on drumbeat pounding in his ears. "So what do I do? How do I stop it?"

Joma seemed to deflate. "I only knew the danger was coming, and acted as fast as I could to stop tomorrow arriving until you could find a solution."

Jack took another swig of whisky and felt himself getting a little dizzy. He didn't know if it was the alcohol, the surrealism of the conversation, or the fact he was dying. "How did you stop tomorrow coming? Tally told me you're a pathwalker, but how do you mess with time itself?"

"By giving up the essence of my soul."

Jack laughed at the drama of the statement, but then he thought about what it meant. "Is that why you're older than you were when I first met you?"

"I'm dying, Jack. Every time the day resets and I hold back tomorrow, I age. Only eight or nine days at a time, but soon I'll run out of life and the spell will break. Put a stop to this, Jack, before it puts a stop to us all. There is a candle in my room that gets smaller every day. It is how I fused my essence into the flow of time and gave myself the power to manipulate it."

Jack looked at Joma. The man was haggard. How would he look in another week or two? "So, to save the world you had to give up your life?"

"It's my purpose, Jack. Many of my ancestors have done the same thing. Global catastrophe is something that threatens us more often than you think, and it always starts with a small-minded group of people with big ideas. I was born knowing that I may have to die before my time. That is the burden my people carry—it is our honour, and our duty. Don't make my premature ending be in vain, Jack. You must find a way to stop this. You have to-"

Jack fell forward from the sofa and onto his knees. There was a burning in his stomach in contrast to the numbness everywhere else. He looked up at Joma and saw the man through a red-hazed filter. "The bite wound on my neck... I'm changing. You have to..."

Joma raised the glass ashtray over his shoulder and brought it down hard on Jack's head.

# DAY 247

JACK SAT UP in bed and cursed out loud. His death had cut his conversation with Joma short just when things were becoming clearer to him. While he had learned many of the answers he had sought, he still had no idea what the hell he needed to do. Joma had said that time was running out and that if Jack didn't stop the virus, it would wipe out the world. It was time to focus.

He went into the bathroom to take a cold shower and clear his mind, and as he lathered himself up, he tried to put the pieces together. If Joma's dreams were to be taken literally, then the person responsible for the outbreak had something to do with... a doll? It also seemed that Tally was somehow involved, and that Donovan had been nothing but an unlucky bystander. Jack himself was only in this mess because his life lacked meaning. He was a lost soul with nothing to lose—a perfect martyr.

Once his shower was over with, Jack got dressed and thought about where to go next. He didn't know how to find Joma during the day, and he couldn't waste time looking for him. They would catch up later at the Voyager Lounge, but until then, his priority was containing the virus and stopping it from infecting the mainland.

There was a knock at the door.

Jack realised what a fool he'd been. With all that was going on in his head, he had forgotten that security would come for him. He had to get out of his cabin, but there would be no avoiding the guards outside.

Jack opened the door and took a swing. He clocked the bearded man on the left with a haymaker and then backhanded the man on the right. Both guards stumbled backwards, but remained on their feet. Jack tried to run by them, but the wispy-bearded guard made a grab for him. He tried to struggle free, but the other guard made a tackle at his thighs and knocked him off balance.

Jack was powerless to resist as his arms were secured behind his back with zip ties. The plastic cords pinched at his flesh, and he could do nothing as the guards hoisted him to his feet and escorted him to the brig.

\* \* \*

They stuck Jack in the same office as before and left him to wait for the captain to arrive. He thought that perhaps he was about to have a golden opportunity to stop the virus. If he could convince Marangakis that a deadly virus stalked his ship, perhaps he would quarantine it and alert the authorities. If the people on the mainland knew what to expect, they might be able to keep the virus under control.

Captain Marangakis entered the room. Jack stood up to greet him, but his offer of a handshake was declined. Hardly surprising, seeing as the man thought Jack was a rapist.

"Captain Marangakis, I know the seriousness of the accusations your waitress, Tally, has made against me, but I assure you they are without merit. She has an agenda, of which I am not yet fully informed, but I would ask that you put her petty vindictiveness aside for one moment and listen to me, because there is something far more important that we need to discuss."

The captain took a seat opposite Jack and looked him in the eye. "What are you talking about?"

"There is a weapon on board this ship—and I don't mean the illegal shipment of arms you have in your hold."

Marangakis leaned back in his chair and seemed surprised. "A weapon you say?"

"Yes, sir. A biological one. Someone on board has released a virus among the passengers. If you take a walk around the ship, you will see that about one third of your passengers have developed cold-like symptoms. By the end of tonight, most of them will be dead, and the entire ship will be infected. Quarantine everyone inside their cabins and keep them there. Tell the French Government to be ready for us when we make port in Cannes. The virus can't escape onto the mainland."

"I don't see what you're trying to achieve, Mr Wardsley, but I will not allow you to cause a panic aboard my ship. My doctor has already informed me of the nasty cold going around my ship, but he also assured me it is nothing to worry about. Your claims are unsubstantiated, and you are just trying to subvert attention from the crime you have committed."

"Allegedly," Jack corrected the man. "Tally has made an allegation. That doesn't make it true. As for Doctor Fortuné, with all due respect, he does not understand what he's up against. No one has ever seen anything like this virus before."

Marangakis huffed. "This mysterious pathogen of yours gets better and better, doesn't it? I suppose you're going to tell me next that it's more contagious than AIDS and deadlier than cancer."

"You don't catch AIDS, Captain. You catch HIV, which develops into AIDS. The virus on board this ship makes AIDS seem like a sore throat. Take me seriously."

"No," Marangakis said. "I will not. This is my ship and you are my prisoner. You will be taken to the brig and detained until I can hand you over to the French authorities."

"Okay," Jack said. "Whatever you need to do, but please just put a call through to the mainland and warn them to take precautions. Tell them I'm a terrorist, for all I care, but take what I'm saying seriously. Please."

Marangakis examined Jack, focusing on his face. He let out a sigh and clasped his hands together. "You realise that if I do as you ask, they will add terrorism to your list of offences. If you make empty threats about a virus on board, you'll be in a great deal more trouble than you are already in."

Jack just wanted to put a stop to the festering evil on board this ship once and for all. "I'm telling the truth," he said. "Just, please, accept the chance I might be right. Warn the mainland."

Marangakis cleared his throat and stood up from his chair. "Fine, but on your head be it, Mr Wardsley."

The captain left the room without further word, and Jack was taken to the cell he was beginning to think of as his.

\* \* \*

The infected attacked the passengers at a little after 20:00 as usual. There was nothing Jack could do to prevent their deaths, but that wasn't the point anymore. This was a 'big picture' problem, and all that mattered was preventing all that death from spreading into the world. Jack hoped with all his being that as midnight came and the ship grew quiet, morning would come and start a new day. If that happened then the future would be corrected and Joma, having seen it was so, would retire his spell. The ship would reach the coast of France with all passengers dead—except for Jack locked safely away in his cell—and the authorities would take adequate precautions to contain the virus. This could all be over in a matter of hours.

# DAY 248

"**S**HIT! SHIT! SHIT!" Jack saw the alarm clock flashing 14:00 on the bedside and smashed his fist against it. The unit shattered and his hand came away bloody, but the pain was nothing compared to the frustration he felt. The best chance he'd had to end this thing had been a failure. Whether the captain had simply ignored his pleas to contact the mainland, or if he had done so and the authorities still hadn't prepared enough to contain the virus, the spell was still in place. Only Joma could tell him why. Only Joma could tell him whether his actions had been worth a damn.

Jack got dressed in a hurry and left before the guards came. He was in no mood to tussle with them today. Every hour he wasted would kill Joma a little more.

He still didn't know where to find Joma during the day, but he didn't have time to wait around until the evening, so he headed for the Voyager's Lounge. When he got there, he approached the barman on duty.

"Hey, there. I was looking for Joma."

The man was polishing a glass with a stringy rag. His English was nowhere near as good as Joma's. "He not here till 19:30, my friend."

"Do you know where I could find him now?"

The man shrugged. "He a quiet man. He keep to himself."

"Which is his cabin?"

The barman gave Jack a suspicious look and placed the glass down on the bar. "I can no tell you that. Speak to him later, here."

"Please," Jack said. "I really need to speak with him. It's important." He slid a hundred euros across the bar, the first time he'd used money since he visited the ship's casino.

The barman frowned, but then relented. "Okay, but you no cause trouble. His cabin C14."

Jack thanked the man and headed for C Deck.

The elevator seemed to take forever to descend, and Jack almost leapt out into the corridor when the doors opened. He was now in the middle of C Deck, and all the lower-numbered cabins were at the fore. Jack headed for number 14, aware that the guards would be searching for him by now.

When he reached the door, he knocked quietly.

There was no answer.

He knocked again harder. "Joma? Joma, are you in there?" He leant against the door, placing his ear against the wood to listen. As he did so, the door swung open. The lock had been busted.

"Joma? Are you okay? Call out if you can."

The room had been witness to a struggle. The television sat at a strange angle, and the room's telephone was hanging by its cord. At the back of the room was a small table where a thick white candle stood as its centrepiece. The wax had melted down to a length of about three-inches, and the flame had gone out. He could tell by the thin trail of smoke filtering from its blackened tip that it had been extinguished recently.

Jack's guts turned over when he noticed the blood on the bed. He took several, creeping steps across the room, following the blood trail that led over to the far side of the bed. He had a bad feeling.

Joma lay dead in a thick pool of his own blood. It seemed to still leak from a deep crater in the side of his head. The murder had been recent.

Jack dropped to his knees beside and shook Joma's body. "Damn it, Joma, you can't be dead. I don't know what to do. I need more time."

Joma opened his eyes. They were bloodshot, unfocused, but they were alive. "Jack..."

Jack couldn't believe it. "Joma! Yes, it's me. What the hell has happened?"

Joma's eyes closed again, but fluttered back open. "T... t..."

"Tally? Are you trying to tell me that Tally did this?"

"T... Tomorrow. You only have... tomorrow."

And then he took in one final gasp before fading away like the melted candle on his table. Joma was dead. The spell was broken.

# DAY 249 - 1400HRS

JACK WOKE UP with a start. Today was his last day before tomorrow. Today was his last chance to save the world. He fought against the urge to stay under the covers and accept whatever fate brought, but he could not allow himself to sit idle while the fate of billions rested in his hands.

Damn Joma for putting him in this position.

If Jack was going to try to stop the virus one last time, then he had to get going. The security guards would arrive soon and they would waste time he could not afford to lose. He headed over to his suitcase and hoisted it up onto the bed. He yanked out half its contents and laid them on the bed. Of the things that lay in front of him, Jack's eyes came to rest on the unopened Glen Grant bottle. The liquid inside sang to him, but he covered the bottle with an evening shirt. Better to keep a clear head.

The next thing he examined was his paperback book. It was crazy—and almost ironic—that in all the time he'd been stuck aboard the Spirit, he had never made it past the first page.

The final thing his eyes fell upon was something he'd almost forgotten he'd brought along with him. The small leather wallet lay open on his bed, a silver shield and crown above a slogan which read: SERVING-PROTECTING-MAKING A DIFFERENCE. On the opposite side of the wallet was Jack's identity card for the West Mercia Police. Once upon a time, the small wallet had meant everything to him, then it had meant nothing at all. Now it seemed to matter again. He'd taken an oath once, to serve and protect the innocent by bringing the guilty to justice. That oath applied now more than ever. Jack was a police officer, and it was his job to do what needed to be done.

He got dressed and left his cabin, knowing it would be for the very last time. He took the familiar elevator upwards and stepped out into the familiar corridor with the familiar laundry cart on his right. He walked towards the Promenade Deck and skipped, mid-stride, as the ship tilted. Outside, he turned to his right and put a hand up.

"Hey! Hey, lads."

The two boys stopped in their tracks, a mere second before they would have collided with him. Jack smiled at them both and said, "You kids be careful now, you hear? Don't want you falling overboard and getting eaten by a killer whale."

The two boys giggled and then strolled away, keeping their speed within sensible levels. It was the first time they'd ever listened to him.

Jack went in the same direction, towards the pool area. He needed to be wary of security looking for him, but there was someone he wanted to speak to one last time. Before he went upstairs to speak to Claire, though, he strolled over to the edge of the pool just in time to catch the young boy about to skin his knee. The boy tripped over his own feet, but fell right into Jack's arms. The mother came rushing over to thank him. With that task completed, Jack headed up to the sun deck.

Claire lay sunning herself beside the empty lounger with the green towel. Jack grabbed the towel, balled it up, and threw it into the sea, watching it sink beneath the waves.

"I... er, think that belonged to someone," Claire said.

Jack sat down on the lounger. "It's been here a long time. Nobody will miss it."

"Did you have to throw it overboard, though?"

Jack shrugged. "I didn't like the colour."

"Fair enough."

"Claire?"

"How do you know my name?"

"It doesn't matter. Just listen to me, okay?"

Claire looked worried but remained quiet.

"Something is going to happen tonight and I want to make sure you and the baby are safe when it happens."

Claire's worried look changed to full on fear. "What? How…"

"I'm frightening you, but it's important you do as I tell you. If tomorrow comes then you'll understand why."

"If tomorrow… what?"

"Be in your cabin by 2000hrs tonight, okay? Make sure you are nowhere near Conner. Conner is sick and so are lots of other people. Stay away from them all."

"You're frightening me. I'm going to call someone."

"You're doing the right thing, Claire. You want to have this baby because you'll be a good mother. I think so, too, but you don't need to be with someone who treats you the way Conner does. You deserve better. You can do it alone, so don't stay with him just because you're scared."

Claire was speechless, but something in her eyes suggested she was taking Jack seriously. She was probably wondering how he knew all of these things about her life, and perhaps that was enough to unnerve her into staying inside her cabin tonight.

Jack looked her in the eye. "In about ten seconds, Conner will turn up and question you about why you're talking to me. Then he will ask you to come with him to get hotdogs. I know this and everything else that will happen today, which is why I want you to stay in your cabin tonight. If you ever want to see Leeds again, you have to lock yourself away."

Conner appeared on cue, and started at Jack. "How you doing, mate?"

"I'm good," Jack said. "I was just about to move along."

"Sounds like a good idea, mate." Conner let out a sneeze then turned to Claire. "Come on, babe. I need you to look after me, I feel well rough. We're all getting hotdogs downstairs."

Claire glanced at Jack for a split second, and he saw the shock in her eyes that his predictions had come true. He just hoped he'd done enough to keep her safe tonight. Because tomorrow was finally on its way.

Jack got up from the lounger and passed by the old couple kissing on the balcony. Despite being sick of the sight of everything repeating over and over, he had to admit there were certain things he would miss. Ironic that he had prayed for the day to end, but now that it would, he was sad to see it go. There was comfort in the things he could predict with certainty. The unknown was terrifying.

# 1500HRS

AS JACK MOVED around the ship, security searched for him. If he succeeded in stopping the virus, he would have a bunch of jumped-up sexual assault charges to deal with once he reached the mainland. Wherever Tally was hiding, she'd have hell to pay if he ever found her. He'd trusted her.

Cared about her.

Jack wondered again if Tally was the one behind the virus. A young Romany girl didn't fit the typical mould of a terrorist, but then who knew what was going on in a person's head? Terrorists could change colour and religion over time, but they were all the same breed of fruitcake in the end. Hatred for humanity was not exclusive to any one kind of people.

After leaving Claire on the sun deck, Jack snuck aboard the Mariner Deck, where he evaded a pair of security guards by stepping through into the Lido Restaurant. Being the largest eatery on board, and open twenty-four hours a day, Jack wondered if the virus had been transmitted via the food here. Was there a way he could find out if anything was contaminated? He looked around the self-service buffet carts, at the trays full of chips, spaghetti, fish fingers, chicken nuggets, beef curry, and many other edibles, and realised that there would be no way of telling. It wasn't like he would find a glowing green pork chop on a bed of pus-filled maggots. He had a matter of hours to do something to help the passengers on board, and prodding through several dozen buckets of cheap food would not be a sensible use of time.

Jack estimated an infection rate of about a third of the total passengers. No members of staff seemed unwell, which made it a safe assumption that the staff-only areas were exempt as possible locations for the outbreak. Come to think of it, he had also seen staff eating inside the Lido Restaurant throughout the day, so that made his theory about the food being contaminated even more unlikely.

Ivor and his family were sitting at a table in the corner. Their little girl, Heather, was sicker than anybody. She might be the key to solving everything. If Jack could find out how she caught the virus, he might have the answer as to how everyone else caught it. Then he might have half a chance to get things under control before it was too late.

He took a seat at Ivor's table. Poor little Heather was as sickly as ever, sleeping restlessly in her mother's arms. Vicky looked ill herself—and mortified—while Ivor wore his usual stern expression that was just a front for a frightened father.

"How are you folks doing?" Jack said.

"We've been better," Ivor replied in a gruff voice. "Who are you?"

"Officer Wardsley." Jack offered his hand. "I understand you're all planning on fleeing to Germany?"

Ivor's jaw dropped. Vicky began to sob.

Jack put his hands on the table and smiled. "Don't worry. No one else knows that you're here. I just wanted to say I agree with what you did, Vicky. Nigel Moot was an evil man and deserved to die. As a mother of a young daughter, what you did was understandable."

Vicky looked at Jack as though she were hallucinating him being there. "T-thank you."

"May I offer you some advice, though?"

"Yes... please."

"Forget about it. Put what you did behind you. If you don't, it will eat away at you until you're a broken mess, trust me. What you did was a moment of madness, but anyone else would have done the same. Don't let it change you. Your daughter needs you."

"Why are you saying all this?" Ivor demanded. "Is this some sort of trick to get my wife to confess?"

Jack placed a hand on Ivor's shoulder. The man's skin was clammy and hot beneath his shirt. "No tricks. I just wanted to tell you I hope everything works out okay."

Ivor said nothing. He studied Jack.

"Your daughter looks sick."

Ivor grunted. "It's just a cold."

"Do you know where she caught it?"

"No. Children often get sick when they travel."

"How long has she been under the weather?"

Ivor shrugged, seemed irritated. "Since last night. We've all been feeling unwell. It's just a cold."

Jack took a moment to think. Last night. Heather got sick the evening they all boarded, which was yesterday. Why hadn't Joma cast his spell a day earlier if that's when everything started? How was Jack supposed to prevent something that had already begun?

He stood up, beaten but not yet down. "One last question, Ivor. There're a lot of people who have come down with the same cold your daughter has. Do you have any ideas about how it could have spread to so many people?"

Ivor shrugged. "I'm not a bloody doctor, man. I suppose, if I thought about it logically, the most likely place to catch a cold is in high traffic areas. Places where people are bunched together. The lifts, restaurants, maybe the tunnel we all queued in before coming on board."

"Hey," Jack said, "you know there's a doctor on the lower deck, right? You should take your daughter down there now to see if there's anything to make her feel a little better."

Ivor nodded. "We were just discussing that."

"Good, the doctor's name is Fortuné. He's a smart man. Goodbye, both. I hope your daughter gets well soon."

Jack left the family alone for the last time.

# 1600HRS

JACK LOOKED AT his watch and grimaced when he realised it was approaching 16:00. Just over four hours until the infection reached its final phase. With each second that passed, it seemed more and more unlikely that Jack would find a solution. He had few facts to go on, and he listed them off now.

Ivor and his family became ill the night after boarding—yesterday.

Ivor's daughter, Heather, is at a more advanced stage of infection—was that due to her age?

Conner is another passenger who boarded the same day as Heather. He's also sick, but his girlfriend, Claire, isn't. She boarded a day earlier. She hasn't caught the virus from Conner, so it seems unlikely the virus is airborne.

Donovan worked for the world's biggest drugs company and was smuggling arms overseas. He was murdered, most likely by Tally.

Tally made false accusations about Jack, to hinder his movements on board. Why? And how did Donovan factor into her agenda?

The ship is at sea and due to dock in Cannes tomorrow. Why did Joma stop the ship today? Why not back in Palma, before the virus was even transmitted in the first place?

Jack was a blind man groping his way down an alley. The answers were in front of him, but he could not see them. Why was it that Claire wasn't infected, but Conner was? Why was Heather worse than everyone else? Where on board was busy enough and cramped enough to infect a third of the ship's passengers?

What was he missing?

"Sir, can you come with us, please?"

Jack turned around to see four of the ship's guards approaching him. They didn't seem like they were willing to talk.

Jack threw a short uppercut to the closest man and threw him into the others. One guard dodged out of the way and threw himself into a tackle, but Jack applied a front face lock and cinched in a guillotine chokehold. It was a matter of seconds before the guard passed out in his arms, but then Jack found himself trapped beneath the man's bulk.

Unable to move, he was helpless to resist arrest as the other three guards recomposed themselves and bore down on him. They hoisted him to his feet and dragged him away. He was on his way to see the captain again.

# 1700HRS

CAPTAIN MARANGAKIS ENTERED the room with the same authoritative display he always did. This time, Jack lacked the patience to show the man respect. He rose from his chair and grabbed the captain with both hands, spinning him around and wrapping an arm around his throat. The two guards in the room were taken too much by surprise to act.

"It's time you and I made a phone call," Jack said, yanking Marangakis towards the door.

"You're in deep trouble, Mr Wardsley," Marangakis said.

Jack squeezed the man's windpipe and made him choke. "Shut up. How do we get to the Bridge from here? We need to contact the mainland. There's something very dangerous aboard this ship, and I don't mean me."

"What are you talking about, you maniac?" Marangakis fought against Jack's arm, but he was going nowhere.

"The Bridge? How do we get there?"

"There's a... there's a ladder outside this room. It leads to an elevator."

Jack dragged the captain backwards into the corridor, keeping his eyes on the guards who were pursuing him. He found the ladder which turned out to be a steep staircase. It led to the ship's surveillance rooms and security offices, and Jack saw an elevator further down. He dragged Marangakis towards it, keeping an eye on each of the doorways as he moved past them. In the furthest security office, the one right before the elevator, something caused Jack to halt.

Tally!

Tally sat in a small room lined with a bank of monitors. She looked bored, inspecting her fingernails. Jack sneered with disgust. She'd pulled the false accusation trick so many times now that she had become tired of having to sit there every day while security looked for him. Accusing a man of rape had become routine and pedestrian.

Tally looked up and saw Jack through the glass pane in the door. Her eyes widened.

Jack prodded Marangakis in the small of his back. "Open it."

"And let you terrorise that poor girl even more? Never."

Jack applied more pressure onto the lower discs of the man's spine, until he cried out in pain. A guard rushed to intervene, but Jack shouted. "Get back, or I'll snap the captain's neck as easy as a twig."

The guard stopped and took a single step backwards.

"Now," Jack said. "Open this door, captain, or I'll hurt you."

Marangakis reached into his hip pocket and pulled out a navy-blue key card. He swiped it against the door and a metallic click rang out as the magnetic lock disengaged. Jack shoved the captain hard in the back, and he fell forwards, head smacking against the thick wood of the door.

Tally leapt up from her swivel chair as Jack entered.

He kicked the door closed behind him and pulled the handle to make sure that the lock had reengaged. Marangakis fled to a corner of the cramped room and turned around to face Jack. His expression was one of outrage. Jack didn't give a damn.

"Stop all this right now," Marangakis demanded. "If you do not-"

"Sit down, shut up. I'm trying very hard to use violence as a last resort, but time is getting too tight for diplomacy."

"J-Jack, what are you doing here?" Tally trembled in front of him, bent at the knees like some frightened child.

"Cut the act, Tally. What's your game? What are you playing at?"

"W-what? Just stay away from me. HELP! God, please help me."

"Leave her alone," Marangakis demanded.

Jack pointed a finger in Tally's face. "She's lying. I never touched her. She's a part of what I'm trying to warn you about. There's a virus aboard this ship, and she knows all about it."

"I don't know what you're talking about. Please, just don't hurt me again. I have a daughter."

Jack took a step towards Tally, veins threatening to burst under the strain of his boiling blood. He almost raised a hand to hit her, but kept his temper under control and instead leant in and whispered to her. "Your daughter would be ashamed of you. That's if you even have one."

Before Jack could gauge Tally's reaction to his words, Marangakis piled into him. Jack's feet tangled up, and he was rammed backwards against the room's desk, where something sharp dug into his back. Marangakis pummelled him with meaty fists, left and right, knocking his vision loose and disorientating him. From the corner of his eye, Jack saw Tally flee through the door while several guards came inside.

Jack struggled to get free, but he was outnumbered. He rolled and twisted, shrugged the captain away from him, but the guards surrounded him inside the small room.

Jack winced and straightened up from the desk. He reached around behind him and pulled loose a blood-soaked pencil that had been embedded in his shoulder. He thought about using it to stab Captain Marangakis, but decided not to. If he injured anyone today, it would be permanent, and like it or not, the people he was fighting were innocent. They didn't deserve to die.

They still needed taking down though.

Jack swung a fist and backhanded Marangakis across the bridge of his nose. Then he reversed the swing into an overhand right and clocked the nearest guard in the jaw. In the narrow space of the room, Jack was able to take down the other men, one by one. In a wider space, they would have overwhelmed him.

Captain Marangakis slumped on the floor, looking like a melancholic Teddy bear. He looked up at Jack and said, "You're a madman."

"Yes, I am, but trust me when I tell you, I'm trying to help you and everyone else. Terrorists have released something monstrous onto this ship and if it reaches the mainland, we're not going to make it. And when I say we, I mean the entire human race. I don't know who's responsible, but the single lead I have just ran out that door. I need to find Tally before it's too late. Don't try to stop me."

Marangakis looked at Jack with zero indication that he believed him at all. Some things just couldn't be accomplished in a single day and convincing Marangakis of the danger aboard his ship was one such thing.

Jack sighed. "Look, just send out an SOS to the mainland, okay? Keep an eye on your passengers, and in a few hours, you'll be wishing you'd listened to me. It might be too late for most of us, but you can still save a lot of people if you send out a warning."

He turned and raced back into the corridor, needing to find Tally before it was too late.

# 1800HRS

TIME WAS RUNNING out fast. Jack raced out onto the Promenade Deck and faced a setting sun above a dark blue sea. If he didn't do something soon, this would be the final sunset the world would ever get to enjoy. He had two hours left, and he prayed to God that Joma's visions of the future had been wrong, because it was feeling like there was no way to stop the virus reaching the mainland.

Jack didn't know how much more he had left in the tank. He was tired and bleeding. His shoulder throbbed where the pencil had speared him, and as he reached his hand around again, he felt the cold kiss of blood against his fingertips. This was one wound that wouldn't be healing itself at midnight.

He headed down the Promenade Deck and passed by a table and chairs. A half-empty bottle of water lay discarded there and Jack picked it up, unscrewing the cap. He poured the tepid liquid onto his hands and rubbed them together, washing away the blood on his fingertips. As he did so, something seemed to click into place at the corner of his mind. As his wet hands rubbed together, Jack was reminded of something from a long time ago, but it was in fact only yesterday. There had been a bearded man at the entrance to the ship when Jack had boarded. The man had been dispensing alcohol rub to all the passengers coming on board.

But it had never been alcohol rub, had it?

Finally, Jack understood how the virus had got aboard. Claire hadn't been infected because she'd boarded the day before Conner. Only Jack's boarding party had been infected, because of the bearded man dispensing the virus right onto their hands. Poor little Heather had got a double dose, thanks to the extra squirt her dolly had received on its plastic hands. Joma's vision of a doll now made sense, but it was of no help. It was too late to help those infected. Poor Heather would turn at 2000hrs, same as she always did. The reason Jack hadn't been infected was because he had dodged past the bearded man and gone straight aboard.

He never had a chance to stop this thing. The man responsible had never even boarded the ship. He was still out there somewhere, hundreds of miles away in Majorca, or even further. He had dispensed the deadliest virus known to man, and would probably release it all over again some place else. Even if Jack stopped the virus on board reaching the mainland, then it might mean nothing, for the virus was already on the mainland—in the hands of a bearded man so callous that he would infect a child face-to-face.

Jack shuddered, but damned if he would play along with a scheme to infect the earth. If killing the passengers on the Spirit was the bearded man's Plan A, then Jack would do his damndest to make sure the sonofabitch had to come up with a Plan B. Hopefully, there would be somebody else to take over once Jack was finished. The world might still have one last chance if he could do what needed to be done in time.

With a dry mouth and a heavy heart, Jack headed for his cabin. There was a bottle of Glen Grant there with his name on it.

# 1900HRS

JACK HAD RETRIEVED the bottle of scotch from his luggage and brought it down to the cargo hold. He'd also brought with him a blanket to cover Donovan up with. It felt good to share one last drink with his buddy who had just been a man caught up in a bad situation, no different than anybody else on board. Donovan was not an innocent man, by any stretch of the imagination, but he was not responsible for anything that had happened since the Spirit of Kirkpatrick had set sail from Majorca. Jack was no innocent man, either. He had been a man consumed by rage, and perhaps always would be, but at least now he had the chance to make up for his past mistakes—to atone for the lives he had taken by saving others. Despite all he had been through, starting with the loss of Laura and ending with what he was about to do this very hour, Jack still valued human life. He was still better than the monsters who had released a virus onto a ship full of passengers.

There were good people on board the Spirit; people like Ivor and his family, Claire, Joma, and Doctor Fortuné. It was for people like them that Jack was willing to give his life.

He took another swig of the whisky and enjoyed the taste one last time. The bottle was almost empty, and he had drunk it so quickly that he was yet to feel its full force. He figured being drunk would make it easier, less frightening.

"Well, pardner," Jack looked down at Donovan beneath the blanket, "if there's an afterlife and you're already there, get me a drink ready."

"Seems like you've already had enough to drink, Jack." Tally appeared from behind the pallet of blue, plastic crates full of cash.

Jack stood up, unsteady on his feet, yet clear in his anger. "I ought to wring your neck."

"Try," she said flatly. "But I promise that this time the bullet will kill you permanently."

Jack looked at the revolver in her hand and recognised it as Donovan's. "How did you get that?"

"What, this?" Funniest thing. When I first... dealt... with Donovan, I took his gun for protection in case you came after me, but I woke up the next day, and it was gone. Guess where I ended up finding it. Right back in Donovan's holster. Weird, because he wasn't under the spell like we were, was he? He stayed dead when I killed him, but I guess the fact that the gun didn't belong with me meant that Joma's spell kept having to make a slight adjustment and put the gun back where it came from. Interesting stuff. Pity Joma's not here to explain it."

Jack shook his head. "Why, Tally? Why kill Donovan and Joma? Why set me up for something I never did? I thought we were friends."

"A friendship forged through fire is brittle, Jack. We are not friends; we are just the victims of fate. My true friends, my family, my daughter, they are waiting for me someplace else. You won't stop me seeing them again."

"What are you talking about? I thought we were both looking for a way to end this. Donovan was, too."

Tally laughed and lowered the gun, but she was too far away for Jack to reach her before she could raise it again. "Donovan wanted to end it, all right," she said. "He wanted to end it all."

"What do you mean?"

"The night Donovan shot you, he took me hostage. He knew all about the day resetting, and that he hadn't truly killed you, but he demanded to know who we both were. We spoke for the rest of the night, and I told him about the spell, and about a pathwalker being on board. It seemed to be a relief to him that there were others beside himself who understood what was happening."

"Of course it was a relief. We were all in this together, or so I thought."

"Me, too, at first," Tally said, "but then I found Donovan drinking himself to death in the Casino one night, and he told me something. He told me he was going to carry on drinking and screwing as many women on board as he could, but that when the whisky stopped tasting good and the sex stopped being fun, he would sink the ship to kill the pathwalker and end the spell. He wouldn't tell me how, just said he had a plan. I couldn't let that happen. I couldn't stand around and wait for him to kill me and everyone else."

Jack took a step towards her. "So you killed him first?"

Tally raised her gun. "And you'll be next if you don't step back. I thought about killing you before now, but I guess I took pity on you and stuck security on you instead. I couldn't risk you finding the pathwalker and making rash decisions. If I could just hold you off long enough, the candle would eventually melt, and the spell would end. Then I could go home to my daughter, along with as much of the cash in these crates as I can carry."

"Is this what this is all about? Greed?"

"No, not at all. That's just a bonus. This is about me being with my daughter again, plain and simple."

"You don't know what you're doing. Joma told me what is at stake."

"I was watching you on the security cameras in the room the captain put me in. Once I knew Joma was the pathwalker, thanks to you, it made things even easier to expedite. Now, the spell is broken, and you and I are going to sit tight until we reach the shore. I will see my daughter again, Jack. Now, back away before I change my mind and shoot you."

Jack did as he was told and stepped back. There was no chance of grabbing her before she could get a shot off. She was in control, and he was getting sluggish from the booze in his system.

"If this ship makes it to land," he said, "the whole world will be wiped out."

"I'm not about to throw my life away and never see my daughter because of the nightmares of an old shaman. Joma could have been wrong."

"That's not true. You were the one who told me about pathwalkers and their abilities in the first place. You told me they were protectors. Joma gave his life so that billions of others wouldn't have to. Your daughter included."

Tally seemed to hiss as she spoke. "I can keep my daughter safe, don't you worry, but I can't do it stuck on this God-forsaken boat."

"You don't get it, do you? The virus on this ship is unstoppable. If it reaches the mainland there'll be no hope for anyone. It's up to us to make sure that doesn't happen."

"I will see my daughter, and you're not going to stand in my way."

Jack glanced at his watch. It was just after 20:00. The infected would attack any minute. The lives of the passengers on board were about to come to an end, and this time it was for keeps. Their deaths had always been inevitable, never any chance to save them. What Jack needed now was to make sure their deaths were the only ones caused by the virus. Tally was the final obstacle in his way of achieving that goal.

It was time to end this.

Jack turned and ran, diving behind pallets as the sound of gunshots rang out behind him. If there'd been any doubts at all that Tally was prepared to kill him, they now vanished. There was no persuading her.

Jack peeked out from behind a stack of boxes and was met by another gunshot. The bullet hit inches away from his face and sent shards of plastic up in the air. Jack crouched down and scurried toward the rear of the cargo area. Tally had said that she didn't know what Donovan's plan had been to sink the ship, but Jack could guess what the cowboy had been planning.

He reached the rear pallets of the cargo area and slid around behind them, using them for cover. Tally had stopped shooting now, which made it impossible for him to pinpoint her location without breaking cover and exposing himself.

He had to work fast.

Jack took out the keys he'd taken from Donovan's body earlier, before he'd draped the man with a blanket. He inserted them into a nearby footlocker now and opened it up to reveal a collection of US assault rifles. Jack had never fired an AR-15 before, but he hoped his military background was enough to help him through. He opened a small green box on an adjacent pallet and pulled out a handful of rounds along with a magazine to load them into. After a quick look over his shoulder, Jack thumbed the rounds into the magazine and slammed it into the base of the rifle with a satisfying clink. He disengaged the safety before pulling the charging handle and priming the weapon to fire. It was time to go to war.

"Don't move, Jack. I don't want to kill you, but I will."

Jack had his back to Tally and was pretty sure she was ignorant of the rifles in the footlockers, specifically the one he was clutching against his chest.

"If you kill me," he said, "then you'll be responsible for billions of deaths, not just mine. Do you really want that, Tally? Is that something you can be okay with?"

"You will not convince me, Jack. I've made up my mind. My daughter is the only thing that matters."

"I was afraid you would say that."

Jack span around and fired off three rounds. Tally flew backwards clear off her feet, as if her body was attached to bungee cords. Her blood soaked the floor where she came to rest on the metal walkway. Her eyes remained focused on Jack, not yet dead.

Jack strolled up to her, kicking away the revolver lying inches from her grasping hand. He pointed the assault rifle at her forehead. "I'm sorry," he said, "but I promise you, this is the only way your daughter will ever be safe."

Tally spat blood at him.

Jack pulled the trigger.

# 2100HRS

THE SOUND OF people being butchered and torn apart on the upper decks was all Jack could hear now. It made him even more resolute about what he needed to do. As an explosion erupted from somewhere above, he thought about Claire and her unborn baby, cute little Heather with her dolly, and the two small boys racing around the Promenade Deck. They would all be dead by now.

He looked down at the six crates full of grenades he'd laid out next to one of the ship's diesel engines. There must have been over two hundred of the handheld explosives, and while Jack was no demolitions expert, he was fairly certain an explosion of such magnitude would be enough to cause a significant breach in the ship's hull. The Spirit needed to sink fast to prevent it being rescued by any nearby vessels. The virus needed to disappear without a trace beneath the depths of the Mediterranean.

There was one grenade missing from the crates. It was in Jack's hand, and he was staring at it in a half-sober haze. The Glen Grant had rendered him pretty inebriated, but he was still clear in his focus and lucid in his intent. From the moment he had boarded this ship, there had only ever been one way of leaving it. He just hadn't understood until now. Whether Joma knew things would end this way didn't matter. It didn't change what needed to be done. The only way the virus could be stopped was if every single person aboard the Spirit of Kirkpatrick died and disappeared. There could be no survivors.

Jack yanked the pin out of the grenade and felt the spring-loaded 'spoon' release into his palm. Once he dropped the grenade into the pile of explosives he would have five seconds. Five seconds of life left to live, five more seconds of pain and grief and anger. It was five seconds longer than he needed.

Jack opened his palm and let the grenade fall. It seemed to roll slowly in the air before bouncing into the crate and coming to rest amongst its brothers.

Jack counted.

"One..."

I...

"Two..."

Love...

"Three..."

You...

"Four..."

Laura...

"Five..."

# THE NEXT DAY

SIXTY-MILES OFF THE coast of France, Commander Harrington looked down from the foredeck of the Merchant Navy bulk carrier, Barstow. The rolling sea of the Mediterranean was littered with debris: passenger belongings, clothing, wooden fixtures of the ship, and pieces of scrap metal. While nothing had been determined yet, it seemed as though the passenger liner, Spirit of Kirkpatrick, had suffered some kind of explosion, perhaps from within the engine compartment. Harrington had been a seaman for many decades and had seen such things before, but not with a passenger ship in modern times. With lawsuits being the way they were, safety checks on passenger vessels were beyond overcautious. It would remain to be seen what the cause was, but Harrington wouldn't be surprised to find out that the explosion was a deliberate terrorist act.

The commander was no stranger to death at sea, but the thought of one thousand passengers and five hundred crew members sinking to their deaths left a numb space in his stomach. Civilians were not suited to terror. They did not embrace it like servicemen did. He pitied the suffering they would have gone through as they realised their time was up. The worst kind of death was one you could see coming—even if only by a few minutes.

What happened to those people? There hadn't even been an SOS. Whatever happened, happened quickly and suddenly. If it had not been for the fact the Spirit had gone radio silent, no one would have even known it had gone down. If Harrington hadn't been in the area, there would have been barely a trace of the ship left. Already, the debris on the water's surface was sinking beneath the waves, removing all trace that a ship had ever floated there. His men were doing their best to retrieve whatever they could before it was lost forever.

Midshipman Brown approached with his trusty clipboard in hand and saluted Harrington from a few yards away. "Commander, we've received word that the French Coast Guard is just a few clicks out. They've requested we hand the situation over to them and that we have their thanks for our quick response."

Harrington smirked. "Typical French. Don't like the British stepping on their toes. Okay, Midshipman, tell the crew we're out in thirty."

"Aye aye, Commander."

Harrington took a stroll along the deck, glancing over his men and supervising the wrapping-up of their efforts. They had divvied up the detritus as best they could, sorting it into separate containers: some containing scrap metal and parts of the ship, others containing personal belongings that could later be claimed by the passenger's families. Harrington walked up to one of those containers now and examined its contents.

There were many things inside: an Andy McNab paperback novel, a jewellery box, and many other mundane possessions. There was even a scorched police badge. One thing that caught his eye in particular, however, was a little girl's dolly. Harrington picked it up and studied its dented face, trying to imagine the child it had belonged to. His heart sagged. The doll was a soggy mess now and seemed to sum up the tragedy succinctly. Its frilly dress had succumbed to the exposure to salt water, and its small plastic hands had gone a sickly green as if some sort of chemical reaction had taken place.

Harrington took the dolly with him and made a personal promise to himself that he would find out whom the toy had belonged to. It would be difficult, because whatever secrets the Spirit of

Kirkpatrick had to tell were now well and truly lost beneath the sea, but he could at least try.

Captain Harrington turned on his heel and addressed his crew. It was time for them to leave. "Let's get back to the mainland, seamen. I don't want to think about what happened here anymore. We've been around enough death and misery for one day. Time to call it a day."

Two hours later, Commander Harrington felt a cold coming on.

## ABOUT THE AUTHOR

Iain Rob Wright is from the English town of Redditch, where he worked for many years as a mobile telephone salesman. After publishing his debut novel, THE FINAL WINTER, in 2011 to great success, he quit his job and became a full time writer. He now has over a dozen novels, and in 2013 he co-wrote a book with bestselling author, J.A.Konrath.

WWW.IAINROBWRIGHT.COM